Phil Murphy
Photo by Karen Atkinson
https://www.karenatkinsonphotography.com/about-k

Goran's Dilemma

PHIL MURPHY

Copyright © 2024 Phil Murphy

The moral right of the author has been asserted.

Apart from any fair dealing for the purposes of research or private study, or criticism or review, as permitted under the Copyright, Designs and Patents Act 1988, this publication may only be reproduced, stored or transmitted, in any form or by any means, with the prior permission in writing of the publishers, or in the case of reprographic reproduction in accordance with the terms of licences issued by the Copyright Licensing Agency. Enquiries concerning reproduction outside those terms should be sent to the publishers.

Although based on a true story, this is a work of fiction. The author seeks to represent authentically historical events featured in the novel, but characters, businesses, places, events and incidents are either the products of the author's imagination or used in a fictitious manner. Any resemblance to actual persons, living or dead, or actual events is purely coincidental.

Troubador Publishing Ltd
Unit E2 Airfield Business Park,
Harrison Road, Market Harborough,
Leicestershire LE16 7UL
Tel: 0116 279 2299
Email: books@troubador.co.uk
Web: www.troubador.co.uk

Cover photograph, The Ada Bridge, Belgrade, at dusk: Milinko Radosavljević

ISBN 978 1 83628 072 9

British Library Cataloguing in Publication Data.
A catalogue record for this book is available from the British Library.

Printed and bound in Great Britain by 4edge Limited
Typeset in 12pt Jenson Pro by Troubador Publishing Ltd, Leicester, UK

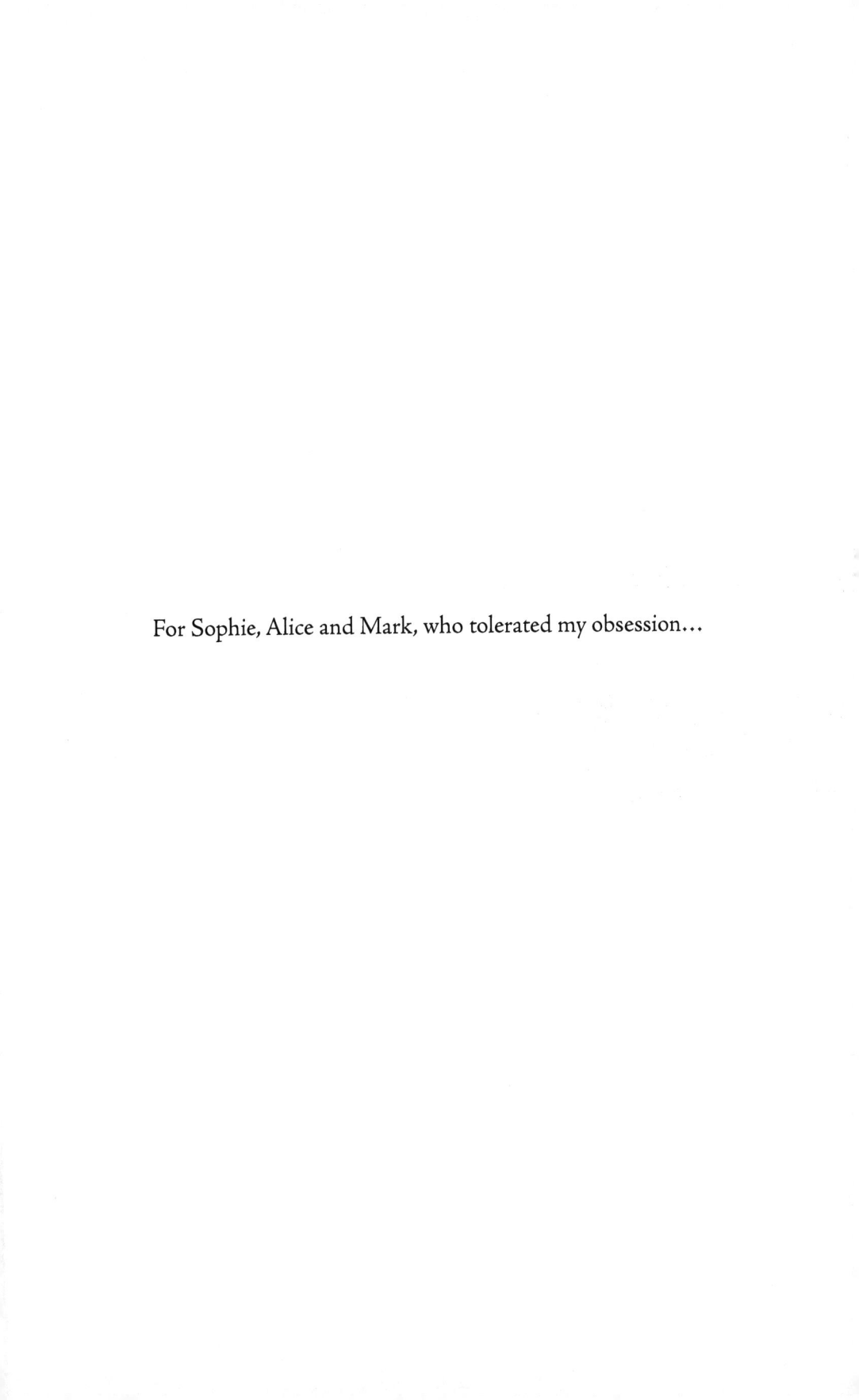

For Sophie, Alice and Mark, who tolerated my obsession…

CONTEXT

This novel opens at a time when Yugoslavia, having suffered just over a decade of economic and social strife following the death of President Tito in 1980, was beginning to pull apart. Political disputes were tipping into military and paramilitary aggression and those holding the heaviest hardware were eyeing up and at times seizing territory from more lightly armed republics with inevitable human cost.

Croatia and Slovenia moved actively to split from the Yugoslav Federation and, when it realised that Serbia and Croatia had designs on swathes of its territory, Bosnia plumped for independence too – to the dismay of its significant Bosnian Serb population.

Two characters at the heart of this novel, Bosnian Serb Commander-in-Chief Ratko Mladić and his daughter Ana, were real individuals caught up in an apparently insoluble contradiction. As best as I have been able, comments assigned to Ratko are based on actual interviews or recordings. There is no record in any location of Ana's words or reflections. I tell the story of the Ratko-Ana, father-daughter axis and its consequences through fictional characters. Some commentators believe that Ana's boyfriend, Goran, was real and did challenge her to renounce her father. Others believe he never existed. He certainly was never identified or came forward. So, in my novel, he is a fictional creation. Milan and Selveta are also fictional creations and the vessels through which I seek to capture the essence of the cruelty and compassion that characterised the conflicts of 1991-5. They bear no resemblance to real people, living or deceased.

I have sought to ensure that the historical and political details are authentic and accurate. For those who wish to understand better the factors that led to the tragic events that brought about and followed the fall of Yugoslavia, I have tried to encapsulate key events and individuals in a series of blogs on my author's Website: www.philmurphyauthor.com

In terms of pronunciation of Bosnian, Serbian and Croatian names, locations and words contained in the book, 'ć' is pronounced 'ty' as in the English tube, 'č' is 'ch', as in cheetah, 'c' is 'ts' as in cats, 'ž' is 'juh' as in azure, 'i' is 'ee' as in keen, 'o' is as in pot, 'u' is like 'oo' in spoon, and 'đ' and its capital 'Đ' are pronounced like 'd' at the beginning of the word dew.

1

She was fathoms deep.

Goran knew that soon he would have to coax Ana gently from sleep, but he chose to leave her a few moments more. Was his continuing to gaze upon her an indulgence, or were the pangs of love that rippled out concentrically from him justification enough? Like prayers offered up to a higher being.

What fuel, what cargo might the brain and the spirit be taking on board in these moments? Clinically, was this absorption strengthening her synaptic transmission processes or putting them under strain? And was the soul at this time taking lessons in soaring, was it feeling weighed down, or did the depth of fathoms allow it to rest, to take relief from the constant questioning that dogs us through all our waking hours?

He knew Ana would awake and speak of how she had barely slept, how she had been awake for hours, but he didn't understand her insomniac claims. Whenever he surfaced, she was always fathoms deep. She might mutter occasionally, but not in words that were decipherable to him. And the topic she would not discuss with him when awake was under lock and key even on the seabed of slumber. He had given up hope of robbing her of her most private thoughts through an act of eavesdropping on her subconscious. It saddened him but – as he suspected she sensed – it put off at least temporarily the moment of truth. Two people can't fall out if there's nothing to fall out about.

Ana was the third woman with whom he had shared the sacred act of sleep. It had been his role in each case to be the partner who led the other back to the surface. It was a profound responsibility, one that he felt, irrationally, carried with it serious risks. What if the slumberer was one thousand miles away in a space that demanded a different kind of consciousness? What if he jolted her back into our world too abruptly? Might the shock be cardiac? His medical training told him that his fear was unscientific, but when did the medical world understand the workings of the spirit? It didn't, and, as he gazed upon the beautiful, submerged Ana, he genuinely feared that a false move might tip her from the ocean bed into an invisible chasm, hurtling her irretrievably towards the hidden core of the planet.

But he had learned techniques. If she were nightmarish, he would gently rub her temple till the demons evaporated; if it was time to get up, either a gentle kiss on the forehead or a warm hand on one of her feet was usually sufficient to spare her from a tumble into the chasm and to float her gently back to the surface, as if he had lifted weights one by one from her garments, like a reversal of the drowning of Virginia Woolf. And he brought tea too – a simple act of generosity that could take the edge off any alarm at too abrupt a re-entry.

"Ana," he whispered. "Time to wake up." He paused. "I brought you tea."

As her eyes flickered and her fierce concentration upon her sleep slackened, the stern demeanour softened and she managed a little smile but, at first, no words.

2

The sense of dread had already kicked in two hours before Goran was due to go round to Ana's flat and then on to the smart Banovo Brdo district of Belgrade for one of their regular Sunday lunches with her parents. Her father, Ratko, was often away 'soldiering', as Goran put it, but, when he was able to return home, Ana liked to visit and Goran felt obliged to accompany her.

As he was getting ready to go and pick up Ana on this occasion, he asked himself more directly than he ever had why he felt obliged to accompany her, given that he felt a discomfort at these gatherings that produced a knot in his stomach that was impossible to untie. He did it, he knew, because he wanted to make it clear to Ratko and Bosa that he was committed to their daughter; that he wasn't some fly-by-night chancer who'd be gone before you knew it.

But there was no doubt that he was uncomfortable in her father's presence. There was a warmth and an optimism in the house when he wasn't there: just Ana, her brother Darko, and their mother, telling stories and talking happily about the children's plans and hopes. When Ratko was home, though Ana clambered over him and cuddled him as she had done as a five-year-old, there was an edge to the atmosphere, as though everyone was tiptoeing around a minefield and someone might set off an explosion at any minute. And though Goran had never been the victim of an angry outburst from Ratko, just taking the odd, sharp jibe that he found impossible to respond to, he reflected on the little details he loathed about him: his way of eating with his mouth slightly open so that everyone around the table was aware of precisely which stage of mastication he had reached at a given moment; the way his belly, lipping over his thick brown belt, spoke of a certain greed; and his endless fidgeting, principally manifested by drumming his fingers on the table or a chair arm to the point at which Goran wanted to scream in irritation. Could he put up with a father-in-law who unnerved and unsettled him so much? Because that was where he, Goran, appeared to be heading.

The thought took him to Ana and he felt a pang in his stomach, which was a regular reaction to his returning to contemplation of her. He loved her so much that he couldn't imagine her ever exiting his life. He had had relationships with other women – not many, but enough to be able to draw some useful comparisons – but this was the first that felt like a perfect fit.

He had known it from the first day he had met her at Belgrade University's Faculty of Medicine. He might have been interested in, even intrigued by, other women before, but now, for the first time, he understood how a partner might make one complete: two pieces locking together to form a whole; the whole greater than the sum of the individual parts. And, after that first meeting, as he walked back to his room not having shown his hand at all to Ana, it was no exaggeration to say that he felt a sense of mild panic: panic that he might not be able to win her; panic that he might not be able to secure her after winning her; panic that, if he didn't act quickly, her magic might cast its spell on another smoother, more beautiful fellow student. The whole love story might be nipped in the bud without so much as a first flowering.

A few months on, Goran had asked Ana whether she had also experienced that immediate chemistry at the time of their first meeting.

"I thought you were gentle and unlike most of the other guys, but maybe I took a bit longer to get the 'chemistry' – or whatever you call it. But that doesn't matter, does it?" she asked.

And though he had a concern that perhaps her comments meant that he loved her more than she loved him, the way she then buried her head in his chest and nuzzled in eased his fears and urged him not to dwell on any doubts.

"Goran," his mother had told him, "there's always an imbalance in a couple's love for one another. One loves more than the other. One needs the other more than the other needs them. But don't worry, because those imbalances change throughout a relationship." And she told him of a girlfriend who had been pursued by a would-be suitor who had written to her every day for a year to prove his love, when she had moved away from their village. She had found him dull, but his relentless campaign to prove his commitment was ultimately effective. "Now my friend has been married to that man for thirty years and *she* is the needy one. She's the partner who's incomplete without him. He's the strong one."

Goran appreciated the advice and acquired a little temporary strength from the story, though he hadn't needed a letter-writing campaign to win Ana's heart.

And his favourite image of Ana firmed up in his mind at that moment. Sometimes she wore her dark brown hair in a shoulder-length bob with a centre parting, but his preference was for her current style: a short haircut with a parting on her left that gave her an elf-like look and made his heart melt when he thought of it or gazed upon it. He felt that it accentuated her big brown eyes, her precisely shaped eyebrows, and the smile that she'd inherited from her mother's strain of the family – shaped like a watermelon slice, revealing perfect teeth. It was a smile that was wide and true and, combined with her sparkling eyes, it spoke of the optimism and altruism that ran through the very core of her being. Goran suspected that he had sensed these attributes from the very first moments, perhaps without identifying them definitively, and that they represented some of the elements in the mix of that personal chemistry that had all but overwhelmed him.

At that point Goran had an ignoble thought. With her father at the centre of the troubles in Croatia and with conflict in Bosnia looking likely, perhaps Ratko, a military leader and a Bosnian Serb, might be killed in action. It was a terrible thought of which Goran was not proud, and he would never share it with or admit it to anybody - Ana especially - but because he had framed it and admitted to himself that he had framed it, instead of chasing it away he conceded that this was a deeply attractive prospect. Not the killing of Ratko; just the simple act of his being removed from the situation. The prospect of a life ahead with Ana without his overpowering presence hanging over them, like a menacing figure in the shadows, felt golden; it felt like it might be a great, great gift.

But he won't be killed, said a voice inside Goran.
He might be, said a contradictory voice.

As usual, Ratko didn't rise from his armchair as Goran and Ana arrived at the house, though Bosa and Darko were up and attentive in the entrance hall. After hugging her mother and brother, Ana went into the sitting room and climbed onto her father, wrapping her arms around him, kissing him, and exclaiming, "Daddy, Daddy! Your little girl's home!"

Ratko hugged her and beamed and chucked her cheek. "How have you been, my little angel?" he said. He acknowledged Goran after a moment, extending his chubby palm and fingers that plumped strangely. They were much fatter in the middle than at the knuckle or the tip, to the extent that Goran had wondered before whether this was due to a medical condition. He forecast correctly that the handshake would once again be as much about virility as it was about welcome. He did his best not to wince.

Goran didn't feel that Ratko disliked him. He felt that he was still being sized up, though he sensed that his parents were perhaps a little too middle class, cerebral and liberal for Ana's father's liking.

Goran knew Ratko's backstory. Ana had even taken him to the tiny hamlet of Božanovići, just outside Kalinovik, south-west of Sarajevo, where her father had been born into a Bosnian Serb family. Fewer than seventy-five people seemed to live there; many of them relatives of the Mladićs. In one house, an uncle had on display on his sideboard a picture of a dashing young Ratko, shockingly lean and with what looked like the magnificent, sculpted quiff of a Teddy boy. Bosa, smiling opposite him in the photo, looked for all the world like Elizabeth Taylor at the peak of her beauty.

And Ratko's relatives told Goran two stories designed, no doubt, to mythologise him; stories that would be repeated at family gatherings year in, year out, whenever evidence of Ratko's exceptional characteristics was required. The first, which Goran believed was pure mythology, was of how, as an eight-year-old minding the sheep, Ratko had spotted a wolf approaching to worry the flock. In a flash, the wolf had grabbed a lamb by the front leg, and Ratko had fastened onto the back two legs. A tug-of-war ensued, and the growling Ratko succeeded in shaking off and frightening away the wolf.

Pull the other one! Goran had thought heretically.

The second story, which did ring true, was of when Ratko first began courting Bosa. Her father had insisted on taking the suitor out into a field and asking him to demonstrate how sound his technique was in wielding a scythe. No point in acquiring a son-in-law if he couldn't help with the harvest, was there?

When Goran heard the story retold by Bosa, she rounded it off each time with the same punchline: "And Ratko passed with flying colours!"

If the village setting was pleasant – rolling hills and stretches of farmland – Goran sensed that the living was dirt-poor, with many of the houses made from panelling rather than brick, their insides grubby, their contents meagre, chickens picking their way aimlessly around the yards, scratching and shitting, completing the picture of penury and decay.

The area had been occupied during the Second World War by Axis forces, and Italian soldiers were billeted in the village when Ratko was born, just months before they would switch sides in the conflict and join the Allies. With Mladić's mother suffering from typhoid and unable to breastfeed him, the baby had only survived thanks to those Italian soldiers patiently feeding him milk and soup.

Mladić's father was not at home because he was away fighting with Tito's Partisans against Germany, Italy, and their puppet Croatian state. On Ratko's second birthday, his father died in a Partisan attack on Bradina in Hercegovina, a village steeped in notoriety as the birthplace of Ante Pavelić, the founder in exile in 1929 of the ultra-nationalist Croatian force, the Ustaše. Pavelić had gone on to ally with the Nazis, leading the Independent State of Croatia from 1941 to 1945. Ratko's father died just months before the end of World War II.

Given his father's Partisan years and the manner of his death, it would have been no surprise that Ratko chose the military life. And Goran acknowledged that, after an upbringing without a father in this unpromising setting, Ratko had at least grafted to claw his way out of a space and a lifestyle that threatened to crush the ambition or imagination of all but the most determined. Nor could Goran overlook the intellect that lay beneath Ratko's seemingly blunt personality. If he cultivated an air of boorishness and, Goran suspected, used that expertly to position himself favourably among competing peers and foes, Ratko had insights, education and articulacy that belied the peasant stock that he wore as his badge of honour.

At that thought, Goran cast an eye for the thousandth time at the bookshelves behind Ratko. Volumes of Gogol, Tolstoy and Dostoyevsky were lined up alongside texts from military leaders, including the Prussian Carl Philipp von Clausewitz's classic work on military strategy, *Vom Kriege (On War)*, and *Memoirs and Reflections* from the hero of the Battle of Berlin that effectively ended World War II, Soviet Marshal Georgy Zhukov. Goran had heard Ratko namecheck von Clausewitz. It had been in a conversation with Darko in which he had suggested that, although *Vom Kriege* was a classic, it was Eisenhower's Normandy landings that were the example of military planning and strategy from which one could learn most. He had namechecked the Serb military leader Živojin Mišić too; a man who had served in every battle involving the Serbs between 1876 and 1918, and won a famous victory over the Austro-Hungarian forces at Kolubara in 1914.

"Darko," Ratko had said, "Serb history is full of political errors and bad judgements that its soldiers had to put right."

It was a comment that Goran would later appreciate as rich in significance, given Mladić's turbulent relationships with his political leaders: Yugoslav, then Serbian President Slobodan Milošević and Bosnian Serb leader Radovan Karadžić. So he was no military fraud, but had he really read the great Russian writers?

"Ana? Those books – Tolstoy and Dostoyevsky. Are they your mother's?"

"Heavens, no. She's never read a book in her life. They're Dad's."

"Has *he* read them?"

"Yeah… I think so."

Goran couldn't bring himself to test Ratko with a reference to Pierre Bezukhov or Rodion Raskolnikov, much as he was tempted.

At the lunch table, the conversation followed its usual pattern: Ratko would begin by talking about the political situation, then decree that no one was to talk politics, only to keep lapsing back into the topic he knew best.

In recent months, Goran had noticed the shift in Ratko's position. Just a year earlier, the man who had joined the Communist Party of Yugoslavia at the age of twenty-two had been virulent in his condemnation of anyone doubting the need or the feasibility of keeping intact the Federation of Yugoslavia. Tito was the man. Brotherhood and unity. And the devil take any nationalist sentiment. But now Croatia and Slovenia were all but gone from the Federation and, before long, Bosnia looked set to plump for its own independence. The Yugoslav National Army, the JNA, once a crack outfit with international respect, was looking increasingly challenged: undermined by desertions and youngsters dodging, or just plain ignoring, the draft. Strategically muddled, it was now often badly led. As Yugoslavia fractured, what would become of it? If Yugoslavia broke apart, surely it was logical that the JNA would break too?

Goran had watched, intrigued yet slightly horrified, as Mladić had embarked upon a process of reinvention, of adapting to what looked as if it would be a very different kind of political landscape. And, over the past year, Goran sensed that Ratko had let his vessel drift on the current until it faced in a completely different direction to that from which he had embarked. No dramatic Pauline conversion; no crash of a lightning bolt from the heavens. Like Slobodan Milošević, Ratko was hoping that his transition from Communist to nationalist would appear fluid and logical when, in his case, it was not only inconsistent with his long-held position; it was also largely driven by necessity.

Goran sensed that, as a man who, throughout his professional life, had known only soldiering, Ratko was preparing himself for a new mission. If he hadn't abandoned his previous convictions, what would he do if they abandoned him? What if holding the Federation together was no longer possible? And if he couldn't change professions, then he'd just have to find a different cause to fight, and hope no one would notice his changing horses in midstream. If Communism's enemies were no longer the enemy, he would have to find another enemy. Otherwise, all his training would be wasted. How might he earn a living? His talk now was less about holding the Federation together and the scourge of nationalism; more about spineless Slovenians, fascist Ustaše Croatians, and the untrustworthiness of "the Turks" – his dismissive term for Bosnian Muslims.

Goran never asked Ratko the questions that he was burning to pose, and he knew, of course, that any attempt to point out the contradictions in his political evolution would prompt a burst of Mladić fury that he, Goran, was not equipped to handle. However, on this occasion some of Goran's questions were answered without his having to risk the wrath of Ratko.

"Darko," Ratko said conspiratorially, "there are going to be some big changes round here." He was trying but failing to suppress a smile that spoke of self-satisfaction verging on pride.

"Oh, yeah? What changes?" asked Darko.

If Ratko was directing the comments at Darko, he was broadcasting his news to the whole table. "Well, don't breathe a word of this to any of your college pals, but over the past few months, they've been reorganising the JNA. Officers who are from Bosnia have been relocated back to Bosnia. Before long, eighty per cent of the JNA forces in Bosnia will be Bosnian – and, of course, mainly Bosnian Serbs. That way, if the Turks try anything, there'll be significant forces to protect Bosnian Serbs and their homes and villages."

"Clever move," said Darko.

"But there's more than that..." Ratko paused. He leaned gently in the direction of his son and, speaking more softly, as if to prevent an imaginary eavesdropper from next door listening in, said, "I took a call from the top brass yesterday... They've asked me to be commander-in-chief of a Bosnian Serb Army."

"What?! The whole shooting match?!" Darko's eyes widened in shock.

"Yes. The whole lot. If it kicks off, we split out a new Bosnian Serb Army from the JNA," said Ratko, now failing to suppress a smile of pride and achievement.

"You said yes, I suppose?" said Darko.

"Of course."

"Wow! Dad! That's fantastic... I knew you'd done well in Knin, but commander-in-chief... Fantastic!"

"Oh, Ratko, you will be safe, won't you?" said Bosa.

"Safe as you ever are in the army, my love."

Goran felt he had better sound enthusiastic. "Congratulations, Mr Mladić. It's a great honour."

"Thank you." Ratko went on to explain that the JNA had consolidated much of its hardware – its guns and ammunition – within Bosnia, so the new Bosnian Serb Army would be "armed to the teeth". With the European Community imposing an arms embargo across Yugoslavia the previous July and the UN Security Council following suit in September, the Bosnian Serbs would be in a strong position "to protect their interests," he said. "That dope Izetbegović – he's leading his Turks towards a cliff edge without so much as a catapult to defend them!" Ratko shook his head as if in disbelief and chuckled quietly at the likely plight of the Bosnian President. "But remember," he said, raising a forefinger and looking round the table. "Not a word to anybody, eh?"

Of course, when he had first met Ana, Goran had been unaware that her father was a military man. What's more, when they had first met, Ratko had been a relatively insignificant player in a theatre that had no war.

Goran's understanding was that Ana's father had had a lucky break professionally in that, shortly after being promoted from colonel to deputy commander of the 9th Corps of the JNA in early 1991, that corps was switched from Kosovo's capital, Priština, to Knin in Croatia. It meant that his unit went from umpiring heightening but, in Yugoslav terms, relatively peripheral tensions between Serbs and the majority Albanian population in Kosovo to a more dynamic role at the very heart of the Croatian War. If it was an anomaly that the area around the town of Knin – the Krajina, or 'Borderland' – was home to around two hundred thousand people of Serbian descent, it was an anomaly that had lasted over five hundred years. Serbs reluctant to be swallowed up by the advancing Ottoman Empire settled west of Bosnia and over time were granted autonomy in Croatia in exchange for forming a tough, hardy human buffer that protected the Habsburgs.

Now Ana's father's unit, though part of a 'Yugoslav' Army, was seeking to convince the outside world that it needed to protect the ancestors of Krajina Serb settlers in and around Knin. In Goran's opinion, from the stories he had told, Ratko had arrived in Knin a year earlier still hoping that the JNA could hold the Federation together, but he had soon sensed that the cause of Serb nationalism was becoming the better horse to back. He seemed to place particular significance in a story that had occurred shortly after his arrival in Knin without ever spelling out why it was important. Goran suspected that this had been an epiphany for Ratko, but that he didn't want to badge the episode as such because that would reveal the inconsistency of his positions.

Around a thousand young reservists, a large majority of them Serbs, had been called up to the JNA and were billeted at a barracks near Kijevo, twenty kilometres south-east of Knin. Ten days after they had arrived, a group of them got hold of a Serbian flag and ran it up the flagpole outside the barracks. In short order, the Croatian military police had arrived and taken down the flag. The following day, the same group of young reservists had unearthed another flag and run it up the flagpole again. This time, when the police arrived the young recruits were gathered around the flagpole and made it clear that there would be bloodshed if anyone tried to take down the flag.

"We're a Serbian Army and we only recognise the Serbian flag," their spokesman had asserted.

Ratko and his superior officer, Colonel Borislav Đukić, had been called to the barracks to defuse the tension and, ideally, have the flag lowered.

Politely, the Serb reservists' apparent leader, an earnest and articulate young man from Novi Sad, explained to Ratko and Đukić, "Sirs, we don't want to break up the Federation but we can see history repeating itself. We can see the Serbs, having made all the sacrifices in World War II, becoming the victims again. We're not breaking up the Federation – the Croats and the Slovenians are – but this time, we won't be the victims."

"Hear! Hear!" his comrades had echoed.

And, Goran noted, Ratko had clearly enjoyed the blood-curdling nature of Colonel Đukić's response: "Comrades! Yes, take down the flag for the moment. But let there be no doubt: if anyone stands in our way, we'll surround them, burn them, annihilate them!"

And, if it sounded like a hollow, meaningless rallying call designed to placate a group of fiery youths, in time those words would prove to have been a chillingly accurate forecast. With reservists from Croatia and Slovenia deserting, Goran sensed that this was the moment at which Ratko had read the writing on the wall. And now here they were, with Ana's father about to lead a new Bosnian Serb Army. From scourge of nationalists to Serb nationalist in one great leap.

From Goran's perspective, as a man enthusiastic about taking the Hippocratic oath, whose parents had taught him the sanctity of human rights, as someone who believed in negotiated settlements, not settlements at the point of a gun, the footage he had seen of Vukovar, Kijevo and Dubrovnik belied Ana's defence that her father was simply protecting the human rights of Serb communities who for centuries had lived in the Krajina and Vojvodina and wished only to continue their lives peacefully.

A few days before their visit to her parents, Goran had risked airing his view: "Ana, I just wonder whether those TV clips suggest that the response from the JNA is a bit…" He paused. "Muscular? I mean, it's not as if Vukovar or Dubrovnik were historically Serb strongholds."

Ana left his comment hanging in the air. It was as robust as Goran was prepared to be at this stage. He knew he had to tiptoe around the subject for fear of being seen to be accusing her father of brutality, a charge that, however accurate it might prove to be, was not something he felt their relationship could necessarily survive at this stage in its evolution and fastness.

He and Ana had already shared their hopes and dreams, even if these were early days. He had suggested to Ana that they spend their early years, once qualified, in field hospitals in Africa; she was of the view that there was significant deprivation and inadequate healthcare in many remote, poor pockets of Yugoslavia.

"Maybe our priorities should be on our doorstep," she had said.

But it was a theoretical debate early in their training, and Goran was just comfortable at having found a soulmate who shared his sense of optimism about the world, who felt that good people could bring about real change. And he wasn't going to jeopardise their relationship because of his misgivings about her father. Well, not yet anyway.

At the table, if there was a mood of suppressed excitement among the male Mladićs, there was still time for Ratko to sour the atmosphere as he picked at his meal with his fork. "So, Bosa, do I not give you enough housekeeping money?" he said gruffly.

"I'm sorry?" Bosa sounded baffled.

"Do you not get enough housekeeping? Can you not afford to buy salt?"

"Of course I can afford salt, my love."

"Well, why have you not put any on this lamb?"

The table fell silent. Goran wanted to stick up for Bosa and her excellent cooking. But he didn't.

"Oh, Ratko. There's plenty of salt in that meal. You'd drown the taste with salt if I let you," said Bosa.

There was still tension in the air. Ratko looked stern – then cracked a smile. Tension eased.

Goran experienced a palpable sense of relief as the door shut behind them and they stepped out into the early-evening air. A couple of hundred yards down the road, Goran said, "So – what do you make of that, Ana? Your dad leading the Bosnian Serb Army?"

"To be honest, Goran, I'm a bit in shock. I don't know quite what to think. It was worrying enough when he was number two in the Krajina, but…" Her voice trailed away.

"Yes, it's quite a move, isn't it?" said Goran.

"Oh, Goran, we'll just have to hope and pray that common sense prevails in Bosnia and it all calms down."

Goran's instinct was that there wasn't much room for common sense, as Yugoslavia careered towards breaking up and political leaders used the rhetoric of protecting their people as an excuse for expansion. But he didn't share his intuition with Ana. He slipped his arm around her shoulder and she looked up at him, tipped her head back, and kissed him.

3

Goran thought fondly of the spacious detached house, set back from the road, in which he and his younger brother had been brought up. In the Senjak district of South Belgrade, where run-down properties, the roar of dual carriageways, and the ugly concrete of flyovers yielded to broad streets, parkland, and residences sufficiently substantial to accommodate foreign embassies, his home was the physical manifestation of an upbringing abundant in security and warmth.

When a teacher at kindergarten had asked him where he lived, he had revelled in the blend of palatals, velars and dentals that the town planner had run together when he had named the street. "Čolak Antina," he would say with satisfaction. And he would be aware, even at that tender age, of the teacher raising her eyebrows, unwittingly acknowledging that this was a child from an affluent area, not one from the poor part of town.

His parents would have abhorred such snobbery – his father was a principal research fellow at Belgrade University's Institute of Social Sciences; his mother was a research assistant – but when he stood on the small balcony above the front door and looked out at the railings around the property, at the stone staircase that led up to the solid wooden door that shut with a weighty click, and at the pillars to either side of the door, he felt safe from an outside world that he didn't understand but he sensed was sometimes chaotic.

His parents apparently effortlessly conjured up an atmosphere for their children that was at once protective and yet open to the currents of the outside world. The presence of two academics under one roof did mean a lot of quiet reading and silent reflection, but Goran and his brother were never afraid to puncture that silence with a question, and

Mother or Father would turn to them attentively and explain or offer a view as best they could. They never resented interruption; they welcomed the opportunity to explain or debate.

"Mum? You know when we were out in town today, why were all those people crying in the streets?" Goran had asked at the age of ten.

"Well, the man who runs our country has died and some people are really sad about that," she said.

Goran knew that the name of that man was Tito, that his picture was in the window of many shops and offices, and that nearly every taxi driver had a card bearing his photograph tucked into their sunshield. "So why did you and Dad not cry when he died?"

When he thought back to the exchange in later years, Goran felt that he had witnessed at that moment a fleeting, unarticulated question passing across her face: *Short version, or long version?* She had plumped for short. "I suppose we feel that he had been ill for a while, he had run Yugoslavia for thirty-five years, and, well…" She paused, and Goran sensed that she was coming to the heart of the matter. "Your dad and I think that we might need a different kind of leadership for our country."

In the years that followed that day, though it was some time before he grasped the politics behind it, the house in Čolak Antina became host to regular evening gatherings of his parents' work colleagues and friends. Goran sensed that the guests might be talking about that "different kind of leadership". Sitting at the top of the stairs as his bedtime approached, Goran would peer through the bannisters at the table in his father's study below. He could only see some of the guests from his vantage point, but the ashtray in the middle, the bottle of rakija, the pot of coffee that had floated its beautiful aroma up the stairwell, and the polite but intense contributions that characterised the discussions all spoke to Goran of adults' business. He was fascinated by some of the snatches of conversation that drifted up to him: "freedom of speech"; "effective communication"; "four-step process of reform". And there seemed to be someone who was very important to his parents and those gathered around the table. They talked a lot about someone Goran thought was called Edvard Kardelj. And they talked too about something called the Praxis Group.

"Mum," he asked the day after one of these gatherings, "who's Edvard Kardelj? And what's the Praxis Group?"

His mother never once told him that it was grown-ups' business that he wouldn't understand. And, after she had explained that Kardelj had been a close adviser to Tito who had ideas about how Yugoslavia might change, and that she and his father were members of the Praxis Group which was working for a freer Yugoslavia, he heard her telling his father about his questions. He sensed from the tone of her voice that she was amused but thrilled by what she saw as his precociousness, though it would be some years before he was able to apply that word to the situation retrospectively.

Goran remembered two further incidents from those post-Tito years. They were remarkable for being two of the very rare occasions on which the atmosphere of calm, civilised, academic debate was punctured and voices were raised in alarm or concern. In each case, only his parents were involved. There were no guests in the house.

Goran had slipped into the kitchen as his father, his voice raised, was saying to his mother, "Mila, some of these guys from the Academy would have us go down the route of nationalism! How can that be?!"

His mother turned her palms upward and raised her eyebrows, as if to say, *Search me!*

Goran knew they were not arguing. His father was rather expressing alarm at an external development – something related to those evening discussions.

A year or so later, it was his mother who was expressing alarm. "Luka, you need to keep your head down. You don't need to be the public face of this. We'll lose our jobs; we'll lose our home!" A rare depth of anxiety afflicted her in that moment.

His father looked down. He made no reply, but from that day the gatherings at Čolak Antina stopped. Goran's parents didn't lose their jobs or their home – but the wars came. The atmosphere in the house was no less protective, but Goran could feel that it was now steeped in feelings of deep sorrow and regret. If forced to characterise the mood, his intuition was that his parents felt that an opportunity had been lost and it would be a long time before it might be realisable again.

Goran's guileless questions stopped. He grew old enough to form his own views, as Yugoslavia careered towards chaos and violence. There seemed little point in alluding to the blatantly obvious. The liberal solution his parents and some of their acquaintances had been mapping out for their homeland had been categorically rejected.

4

A few weeks after Goran and Ana had had Sunday lunch at her parents' home, they were back there again at short notice for an impromptu barbecue. Ratko was in town with some army colleagues and there was time for them to swing by for a modest celebration. The sun was shining and the guests were gathered on the lawn by the side of the house.

Goran had been relieved to see upon arrival that there were sufficient guests – extended Mladić family, some local friends, as well as around half a dozen JNA officers in uniform – to enable him to loiter on the fringes of the party and to keep his own counsel without being seen to be rude or uncomfortable. He looked out from the front edge of the lawn and wondered whether, from the second-floor balcony at the front of this grand, three-storey house, he might be able to see where the southern outskirts of Belgrade opened into countryside. He had not yet been invited onto that balcony.

Ana was helping to prepare food and, though he would have been happy simply to have nursed a beer or two and slipped into the comfort of his own thoughts, when he spotted a young officer also on the fringes of the gathering and, unlike the other JNA cronies, not involved in the process of ingratiating himself with Ana's father, Goran latched onto him. The young man might provide him with cover for his reluctance to be drawn into the gaggle. Although Goran couldn't let on that he was aware of the imminent military reshuffle and Ratko's elevation, he could sense that among the officers endlessly and annoyingly joshing one another, there was an awareness that their host was about to become the Bosnian Serb Army's main man, and would, therefore, be allocating shortly some plum posts.

Goran offered a hand. "Hi – I'm Goran. I'm the boyfriend of General Mladić's daughter. Pleased to meet you."

"Hi – I'm Milan. Milan Tešević, 9th Knin Corps. I'm an adviser to the general. Well… informally." His handshake was firm without trying to make any pecking-order point.

Milan's uniform was a simple combination of shades of which any fashion designer might have been proud: a sage-green jacket with four square front pockets and four buttons; a thick brown belt; a perfectly pressed pale green shirt; and a plain, dark olive-green tie. He was holding a cap pinched flat bearing the Yugoslav red star badge. Up close, Goran was struck by how much younger Milan was than the other officers in the Mladić entourage. He could barely have been in his twenties, and although he, Goran, may have been just a couple of years older, Milan seemed schoolboy-young. Goran wondered whether he might be teased or even bullied in the macho environment of the army. Just one word summed up a number of Milan's attributes: sallow. It wasn't a word Goran required frequently, but now it leapt into his mind. Pale skin, straw-coloured hair too light to be deemed blond, and blue eyes at a point on the spectrum proximate to grey, as if colour had been drained from his crown to his chin. Yet his was not an unhealthy sallowness. He was slim and lithe, and Goran felt he was not being overanalytical in reading in those eyes, despite their pallor, the keen intelligence behind a high IQ and an emotional intelligence that perhaps belied Milan's tender years.

"Ana and I – we're students at the Belgrade Faculty of Medicine." Goran was fumbling for conversation but, once out, he realised his comment was designed to differentiate himself from the Mladić bloodline, even though this was a man he had never met and may never meet again.

"I don't know her – but I've seen her here this afternoon. She's a pretty girl," said Milan. "You're very lucky."

"Yes… Thanks," Goran said. He realised that small talk would detain them only for a few moments. "So, how's soldiering? You out in Knin with the general? It sounds pretty hairy out there."

"Yes – I've not been there long. Been fast-tracked from military school in Zemun to join the general's advisory team. From the classroom studying military theory to the front line." Milan gave a weak laugh. "Mind you, it's a privilege to be learning at the feet of a master." He jerked his thumb in the direction of the main group, absorbed in an adulation of Ana's father that dare not overtly speak its name.

"You mean Ratko?"

Milan nodded.

"So he's a good leader, is he?"

"They say he's the best. I've not been with him long but the rest of the boys – they love him. And from what I've seen of him in action…" Milan paused, perhaps for effect, then said in hushed tones, as if in awe, "masterful – quite masterful!"

Milan had been told by older hands that, whereas other generals would shout, "Charge!" and order their men out over the top, Ratko would lead by example, leaping out of the trench and shouting, "Follow me, men!" He would bivouac overnight with his men on the front line, challenge them to games of chess in downtime, and offer a shot of home-made rakija from his hip flask to even the youngest starstruck recruit.

And Milan cited a recent episode near Vrlika, just thirty kilometres south-east of Knin, as an example of the general's bravery and leadership skills. With the Serbs having declared the Krajina an autonomous area within Croatia, Croats looking to limit the scale of their expansion over the area had blocked the main road with a single-decker bus and planted an explosive device in it that would detonate if anyone tried to drive it away. When Mladić arrived on the scene, he had expressed exasperation at the local militia, fearful of booby traps, who were calling for the Bomb Squad rather than examining any device, said Milan.

"He said, 'If you don't go and take a look, you don't know what you're dealing with, do you? No need for the Bomb Squad if it's just some pissy device a few Croat amateurs have put together.' And he asked someone to fetch him some pliers from our jeep."

As Mladić had climbed into the bus, one local journalist who had turned up after a tip-off about the incident had said, "He's a fucking madman. I've seen this sort of thing in Jerusalem. The whole thing could go up."

Milan said that the seven or eight minutes that Mladić spent on the bus felt like half an hour. "Everything was silent apart from birds twittering in the trees. I was expecting an explosion to rip through the air at any minute. And then he emerged, holding some wires. He said, 'All done.' And he looked at the head of the militia and said, 'You, or one of your guys, can jump-start the engine and drive it off the road now. It's perfectly safe.' It was an order, rather than a suggestion."

Milan said that the lead militia man had looked nervous, and the journalist had asked Ratko which wire he had cut. "Ratko said, 'The yellow one.' The journalist asked him how he knew that that was the right one to cut. 'I didn't,' said Ratko – and he turned and headed back to the jeep." Milan chuckled as he completed the story. "Fearless," he said. "Utterly fearless."

But if the story of the device on the bus cast Ratko as a larger-than-life, near-pantomime character, Milan's next story lifted the veil on his more ruthless side. Milan explained that, while local militia and the 9th Corps had rendered the town of Knin, the Krajina's de facto Serb capital, pretty much impregnable, settlements beyond the town could occasionally be rocked by shells launched from Croat villages.

"The general has a simple rule: 'If one of our guys is injured, our men go in and kill ten villagers; if they kill one, our men kill fifty.'" Milan recalled how 9th Corps men had been ordered into one village and had made the village elder hand-pick nine villagers to be put to death. He explained that the tenth killing was reserved for the village elder's wife – though the elder himself was spared so that he could suffer his loss 'properly'. Milan winced at the recounting.

"That's a bit brutal, isn't it?" said Goran.

"Well, it's the only way to teach people that we won't tolerate being taken for sitting ducks."

Goran heard Milan's words and he sensed a touch of swagger in the telling of the story, but Goran didn't believe that Milan had taken part in any of these revenge missions and his reading of this young man was that it was not behaviour with which he was comfortable. It seemed that the emotional intelligence he had divined in Milan was being crowded out by a rookie's hero worship of the general – temporarily, Goran hoped.

Goran thought back to Milan's introduction. He had said that he was an adviser to the general – "well… informally". Goran suspected that that qualification meant that the likelihood was that Milan *wasn't* his adviser. Perhaps when he had first landed in Knin, Ratko had chatted to him in the officers' mess, made him feel respected, plied him with gratitude for supporting the cause. Whatever had happened, Milan was clearly in thrall to him and Goran sensed that it might be some time before that spell was broken and Milan's innate sense of decency prevailed.

It transpired that Milan came from a liberal family not dissimilar to Goran's, but while Goran's parents had sought reform from their academic platform, Milan's father was a journalist on the independent *Borba* ('The Struggle') newspaper and had taken not inconsiderable risks in trying to maintain balanced reporting in the turmoil of post-Tito Yugoslavia. Remarkably, *Borba* had somehow navigated the Press restrictions that had closed many publications in Serbia and was still hitting the streets even after the outbreak of the Balkan conflicts with its message of the folly and dangers of Serb nationalism. Goran wondered though whether Mr Tešević sometimes feared a knock on the door.

"I was studying journalism myself before I was called up and given an officer's commission," said Milan. "Dad wasn't crazy about my taking it up. Said I should just keep my head down, serve my time, and get out. But I told him I wanted to see what it was really like on the inside of the military – not just peer in from the outside. Might make me a more authentic journalist afterwards." He paused. "I'm not regretting my decision."

Goran wondered whether Milan really believed that, or whether he was having to talk up his enthusiasm.

As the conversation meandered, it led, predictably, to football chat; then, less predictably, to the revelation that literature was Milan's great love. Goran could sense him relaxing. Yugoslavia's break-up and military matters were clearly not subjects for which he had any great passion. By contrast, Milan quickly but unostentatiously demonstrated the breadth and depth of his reading and his appreciation of great writing. Steinbeck, James Joyce, Stendhal – he had read them all in translation and, Goran suspected, could have talked away the rest of the afternoon discussing them, had Goran's acquaintance with the literary giants been more extensive.

"Did you know that Ana's old man has a shelf full of Tolstoy, Chekhov, Dostoyevsky, and Gogol in there? I thought they might be there for show, but Ana tells me he's read them," said Goran.

"Really? Well, that does surprise me," said Milan. "I didn't have him down as a literary man. I'll have to ask him about that."

Goran momentarily regretted sharing that intelligence. Might he be fuelling further Milan's admiration of the general, he fretted? Then he swatted away the concern. The conversation had demonstrated that his first instincts about Milan were accurate and that a sharp intellect, sensitivity, and emotional intelligence all lay within this admirable young man. Goran had to believe that these attributes would assert themselves over time, and that Milan would not be capable of justifying for long the actions of a man comfortable with ordering the death of a village elder's wife.

Ana emerged, moved in between Goran and Milan, and slipped an arm around Goran's waist. He smiled at her.

"Ana, this is Milan. He works for your dad in Knin."

Milan offered his hand. "Pleased to meet you. I'm one of the team of comms advisers in the 9th Corps."

Goran's conversation with Milan had fulfilled the ambitions of anyone tempted to throw a party: it had brought together two people who had never met before and left them at the end of the event feeling enhanced. So it didn't feel anything other than natural for Goran to swap contact details with Milan and ask him to look him up whenever he was back in Belgrade.

"I wouldn't recommend it at the moment, but if ever you're on a road trip through Knin, look me up!" said Milan, and he laughed, providing Goran with a gauge of just how much Milan had relaxed in the course of their conversation.

When he looked back on that exchange years later, after all that had happened to both of them since, he couldn't be sure, but Goran did wonder whether part of the swapping of contact details was a vague sense that this was a young man who, because of his proximity to Ana's father at a working level, might somehow provide part of the solution to the puzzle of how he might extricate himself from his association with Ratko, while emerging with Ana still on his arm.

As Milan was driven off with the rest of the JNA entourage as the party wound down, Goran turned to Ana.

"Nice guy," he said. "Too good for the JNA!"

Ana gave him a playful pinch.

5

A few months later, the contagion of war had spread to Bosnia and threatened to suffocate it. As in Croatia, this wasn't orthodox war: one big army lined up against another. Conflicts would flare up across towns and districts, accounts carried on the wings of rumour and refugee from areas often too dangerous for journalists to reach.

But although Belgrade kept a tight grip on public broadcasts, Goran and his college friends could easily tap into CNN or the recently launched BSkyB satellite channel to get from independent journalists some sense, however patchy, of what was happening on the ground. He had watched in horror as Sarajevo had been besieged after Bosnia voted to follow Croatia and Slovenia out of Yugoslavia's Federation and Bosnian Serb political leader Radovan Karadžić had warned that, if it tried to go it alone, Bosnia would "disappear". Surely the superpowers would step in? Apparently not.

For Goran and Ana, there were personal developments in parallel. As the conflicts spread and Goran sensed that Ana realised that her father would be drawn ever more centre stage, they were becoming ever more intertwined as a couple. There was an irony inherent in the fact that, at the same time as he loathed the way in which Yugoslavia was tipping into more and more violent conflicts, loathed the role her father was playing in the 'process', Goran and the general's daughter were binding together more tightly than even he could have hoped for. Hate the man, adore the daughter. Hate the man, be adored by the daughter.

He wasn't sure how aware of it she was, but he was conscious that every projection she made, every life plan she mooted featured them in tandem. She didn't talk of marriage; there was simply an unspoken assumption beneath every conversation that they would always be together – personally and, most likely, professionally too. Goran couldn't quite pinpoint when this had first taken form, but he hoped that what she was latching onto was a solidity and a reliability that he aspired to epitomise. Moral substance nurtured by his parents, constancy in a Balkan world that appeared to have gone mad, but above all – the glue that bound everything together – deep, unquestioning mutual affection. She never talked about what was happening on the ground in Croatia, in Bosnia, in Sarajevo, and in the corridors of power in Belgrade, but he could feel her need for someone to cling to in bed; her need for unstinting support, but one that came without commentary on current affairs. He struggled to keep commentary mode on pause, and he felt that there might come a point at which he would have to speak out… but it wasn't now. Though there was the odd lapse.

After the siege of Bosnia's capital had begun and innocent Sarajevan demonstrators marching for peace had been shot dead by snipers, after parts of the city had been pulverised by Bosnian Serb bombardments, there had been a showdown in a street near an army barracks and Yugoslav Army soldiers had been gunned down by local militia. It was the first time Goran had heard Ana use the vocabulary of her father.

"Those fucking Turks!" she had screamed at the television set. "Forty-two good men murdered. Bastards!"

Goran wasn't sure how he had spoken so calmly, but he had replied, he hoped without emotion, "Ana, CNN are saying there were six fatalities, not forty-two. And you know, the JNA did bombard Sarajevo the day before and kidnapped the Bosnian President. Are we surprised that there was some kind of backlash?"

They fell silent. Goran sensed that they both regretted their outbursts. They reset to 'pause commentary' mode.

But the episodes that had prompted them to break their silence – the JNA deaths, and the kidnapping and then safe release of Bosnia's President, Alija Izetbegović – led to the reorganisation that Ratko had previewed at the lunch table some weeks earlier. The anomaly of a 'Yugoslav' National Army playing a role in the bombardment of Sarajevo could no longer hold. In an operation captured on film, the JNA pulled out of Bosnia almost ceremonially, though many of the Bosnian

Serbs from its ranks were simply rebadged and transferred into a new Bosnian Serb Army that inherited much of its predecessor's hardware and apparently inexhaustible ammunition stockpile. And Ratko was its commander-in-chief. From the relative remoteness of Knin and the 9th Corps' largely unreported activities there, it seemed to Goran inevitable that Ana's father's profile would increase; that he would go from being a niche character, known only to those steeped in military matters, to a public face of Bosnian Serb aggression towards the cosmopolitan citizens of Sarajevo – a city renowned historically for its multi-ethnicity and its tolerance.

Goran both forecast and feared a shift from backwater to international notoriety. He wrestled privately with the clanging, jarring contradictions between what the public witnessed on satellite TV as sections of Sarajevo were reduced to rubble, and the oaths that he and Ana would swear once they were admitted as full members of the medical profession. He recalled only snatches of the Declaration of Geneva that was the principal successor to the Hippocratic oath. He would have to pledge solemnly to consecrate himself to the service of humanity. He would not permit considerations of creed, ethnic origin, nationality, or political affiliation to intervene between his duty and his patient – and he would make these promises 'solemnly, freely and upon his honour'. And Ana would too. He knew that these were the very type of values that had driven her choice of a medical profession; he knew that she believed in the principles underpinning that oath absolutely. But the thought gnawed at him persistently: it was incompatible to swear that oath and fail to renounce a father who was so deeply implicated in the killing game.

Sometimes he would plead privately for his conscience to leave him in peace. *I know, I know, I know.* His inner voice would torment him, as if his conscience were personified and was in debate with himself. And occasionally he would frame the defence that it was Ana's issue, not his. But as soon as that thought began to gain shape, he would realise that it was untenable. If they were becoming inextricably intertwined, soul bound to soul, it was his issue too. It would have to be addressed.

And as the siege ticked on, the situation worsened, as he had forecast. Ratko was not just drawn into the frame; he appeared to revel in notoriety.

After BSkyB screened footage of what was reputedly the heaviest night of bombing of Sarajevo to date, the night sky lighting up for hours with explosion after explosion, the Bosnian Government handed the broadcasting companies recordings intercepted by their security services of the person who had directed the onslaught. Goran recognised it as unmistakably the voice of the new Bosnian Serb commander-in-chief, Mladić. He ordered missiles to be targeted at the Parliament and the Presidency Buildings, but even Goran was shocked when he heard Ratko call for the Velešići residential area of the city to be shelled.

"Shell Velešići – there aren't many Serbs living there," he had cried. The implication was clear: it was okay to kill some fellow Serbs provided you kill a whole lot more Muslims at the same time. And Ratko had continued, as if in a frenzy, "Shell them until they're on the edge of madness!"

The BSkyB footage of some of the victims of the night's bombing arriving at hospital – all ages from young children to the infirm elderly – was barely watchable, yet, when confronted with the contents of the leaked tapes, Mladić was in no way chastened. One TV reporter said he had told him that he held Sarajevo "in the palm of his hand", and he bragged openly that the world was so transfixed with what was happening in Sarajevo that it couldn't see what else he was doing across the rest of Bosnia. As would emerge later, the reality was that his forces were mopping up around two-thirds of Bosnian territory. Goran knew that any claim that Bosnian Serbs were merely reclaiming the two-thirds of Bosnia that were historically Serbian was utter nonsense.

As the weeks passed and any talk of peace plans or intervention appeared to lack conviction, Goran took the initiative of dropping Milan a line, expressing concern for his well-being in this new situation. It had gradually dawned on him that his and Milan's putative friendship would go nowhere – indeed, it would wither away before it had had oxygen to grow – if he didn't take the first step. And, as he framed his short note, it struck him that, while he did want intelligence about Ratko's professional activities and behaviours, he also genuinely had concerns for Milan and hoped that he would find a space in the army that was tolerable, if not comfortable.

It was some weeks before he received a reply, but he was quietly thrilled when he realised the letter was from Milan. His neat handwriting spoke of a young man accustomed to putting down his thoughts on paper – something of a rarity these days, Goran reflected. And Goran wondered whether sensitive, sallow, bookish Milan might struggle to find opportunities to make new friends and so was enthusiastically seizing this offer from him to forge a bond. One thing he was confident about was that, through the process of having written to Milan and received a reply, they were establishing a relationship which would see them through to a place beyond the conflicts currently dogging the now 'former' Yugoslavia at least, and most likely well after that.

Milan's news was not encouraging, as he had found challenging the relocation from Knin to Pale, twenty kilometres south-east of Sarajevo, where the Bosnian Serb Army was now based. Goran read between the lines that, for Milan, the gloss had not yet rubbed off General Mladić. He was 'decisive and strategically clear', according to Milan, but he admitted he didn't quite understand the rationale behind the siege, and when he was close to the action he found the scale and relentlessness of the explosions 'trying'. Goran wondered whether he really meant 'distressing'. 'It's a powerful experience, particularly being so close to the leadership, and I'm sure it will give me much material to write about after the conflicts die down, but I'm not convinced I'm cut out for the military life. I dream of withdrawing to a remote island and writing my novel!' Milan wrote.

There was some good news: he had been given a promotion, after the Bosnian Serb Army and administration realised that the Bosnian Government was running rings round it in terms of selling the story of their people's plight to the outside world. Now Milan, with his rudimentary journalism training, was being asked to try to rectify some of the imbalance and get the message out that the Bosnian Serb Army was endeavouring simply to protect Serb communities in Bosnia in the face of attacks from Bosnian Muslim 'terrorists'. 'Izetbegović's people have employed multi-million-dollar US PR agency Ruder Finn to promote their story; Ratko's Army has got me!' Milan wrote.

The phrase 'putting lipstick on a pig' flashed into Goran's mind, but Milan said that he was cultivating some Western journalists and was hoping to get them to run stories highlighting the slaughter of innocent villagers in several Bosnian Serb areas near the border with Serbia, perpetrated by Bosnian Muslim militia. 'I've got an idea too to put some select journalists in front of Ratko and try to persuade him to be on his best behaviour. Talk about some of the bad guys shelling our positions and our people,' he said.

Milan signed off, wishing Goran and Ana well. Goran folded the letter and put it into the desk drawer in which he stored the letters from Ana and from others that he wanted to keep.

6

Some weeks later Goran awoke to headlines that he feared might have chilling implications both for Ana and for Milan. 'Bosnian Serb leader threatens to bomb Washington and London,' the headline read. The strapline beneath read, '"Just one match" jibe from Mladić.'

A journalist from *The Times* of London had landed the scoop in an exclusive interview with Ana's father. Goran winced with concern. It sounded like one of the interviews that Milan had hinted he might seek to arrange with 'select Western journalists'.

How could it have gone so spectacularly wrong? Goran asked himself. The answer came back to him instantly: *Park Ratko in front of a serious journalist and you're just inviting him to say something brimming with bravado and menace.*

The story was based on Mladić being asked whether Serbs might take action beyond the borders of Bosnia in the event of armed foreign intervention.

"One furious Serb can do a lot of damage with just one match," he had replied. Asked whether that might be a threat perhaps to detonate a bomb in London or Washington, he had replied, "The Serbian diaspora reaches all parts of the world."

Goran didn't know whether his drawing Ana's attention to the headlines constituted a breach of the 'no commentary' rule, but he needed to be sure that she was aware of the story that had broken before she stepped into the outside world that morning.

She barely reacted. "These journalists, they're always making stuff up. It's rubbish."

Goran said nothing.

A couple of hours later, the phone rang in his flat. It was Milan on the line. He sounded chirpy. "Goran, I'm back in Belgrade at the weekend. Are you around?"

"Well, yes, sure. It'd be great to see you but…" Goran paused for what seemed like a long time but was probably just a few seconds. "But aren't you in trouble? I mean… that interview. Has the shit hit the fan?"

Milan laughed sharply at the other end of the line. "No, no. Ratko loved it! I think he thinks it makes him an even bigger international figure. He's famous! And though it's nonsense, that kind of stuff goes down really well with the rank and file. They think it's great."

"Oh," said Goran. "When I saw it, I thought it was bad news for you."

"It wasn't quite what I had in mind when I put *The Times*' guy in front of him, but, well, Ratko thinks I did it on purpose. Teed him up to ask the question. I didn't, but now he thinks I'm a PR genius! Anyway – enough of that. Shall I see you on Saturday?"

"Yeah, when?"

"I'll come to your place for three. We can have a couple of beers and I'll tell you all about it."

Milan hung up. Goran shook his head in disbelief.

When Milan turned up, Goran was shocked to see him in a maroon crew-neck top, jeans and trainers, rather than how he appeared in his mental snapshot of Milan: in shades of military green. These civvies softened Milan's sallowness to a degree, though it would be an exaggeration to suggest that they suffused him with any rosy glow.

Quite quickly Goran divined that, psychologically, Milan was tiptoeing along a ridge, on one side of which lay thrill and on the other lay anxiety. He seemed at one moment to be flushed with a warmth that Goran interpreted as the confidence born of promotion and greater professional responsibility. In the next moment he sounded troubled by a working environment that he never would have chosen and, if permitted, would quit in an instant. His role as spin doctor also seemed to be prompting him to parrot more Bosnian Serb lines, apparently unashamedly, but when Goran dug deeper he found it relatively easy to expose Milan's misgivings about the bluntness of the military exercise and the long-term viability of its goals.

Milan explained how by chance he had come across a young English journalist, Mick Morrison from *The Times*, in the Premier Café in Knin. Mick had been on his way down to Dubrovnik, having got wind of the imminent siege of that city in the early months of the conflicts in Croatia. "He was only a bit older than me. Seemed a bit raw – but he didn't have that cynicism that a lot of the older hacks have. I just got a sense that, even if he was more likely generally to side with our opponents, he'd listen to our message and report it straight. Quite frankly, I liked him and I trusted him." Milan reported a degree of pushback from Ratko when he had suggested the interview with Mick. "I'd shown him some of his articles and he said, 'Oh, he's written the same anti-Serb shit the rest of them write. I'm not speaking to him.' But I persuaded him that Mick would report straight what he said to him. So we just had to be clear about his message. He said, 'Okay – but if he fits me up, you're for the high jump.'"

Milan had prepared *The Times*' journalist in the bar of The Two Doves hotel on Karađorđeva Street in Pale the night before the interview. "He'd done his research. He'd talked to other journalists who knew Ratko and, though he was excited by the exclusive I was offering him, he was clearly nervous. He said one colleague had mentioned how Ratko revelled in notoriety, so he didn't mind stories about how ruthless he could be, but another had warned him Ratko could turn in an instant – maybe even grab a journalist by the throat. I told him he wouldn't do that if I was in the room, but I could feel his tension the following morning when we were waiting for Ratko to turn up at our Army HQ."

Milan said that a few days earlier he had sat through a two-and-a-half-hour session between Ratko and a former British Foreign Secretary who was trying to cut a peace proposal, Dr David Owen. "I know Ratko likes to come across as – how can I put it? – rough-hewn, maybe."

"He cultivates that. I think he thinks boorish is attractive," said Goran.

"Well, if you'd heard him, you'd have been well impressed. Over those two and a half hours, he laid out in detail Serbia, Croatia and Bosnia's strategic needs, core tactics, and military and political strengths and weaknesses. You could see Owen was impressed. I'm not saying he warmed to Ratko as a human being but he'd met Radovan Karadžić before and you could sense that he realised which was the expert and which was the amateur, the playboy."

Milan said he was hoping *The Times*' man might capture some of the in-depth knowledge and some of the subtlety of the Mladić character, but his and Ratko's main aim was to have him report on some of the atrocities perpetrated by Bosnian Muslims' most notorious 'terrorists', so that the outside world could understand why the Bosnian Serb Army was taking such a vigorous approach to protecting Serb communities in Bosnia. They had started well by Mladić responding enthusiastically to Mick's Irish antecedents.

"Morrison – it's a very Irish family name," Mick had said.

"Ah, the Irish! I like the Irish – probably because they're another downtrodden nation. The Serbs and the Irish – we could tell each other some stories. We've a lot in common."

Ratko had then gone on to ask Mick if he had heard of Naser Orić.

"He said he hadn't, and Ratko explained to him that Orić had been a JNA man who had risen to the point at which he was one of President Milošević's personal bodyguards. But as a Bosnian Muslim, he joined Izetbegović's gang when the JNA broke up, and he became a big cheese in and around Srebrenica," said Milan.

Ratko had told Mick that the charge list against Orić was long: multiple innocent men, women and children had been murdered in cold blood by him and his men, culminating in the massacre of sixty-nine people from Zalužje and other villages in the Bratunac-Srebrenica area on the day Orthodox Serbs celebrated the Feast of Saints Paul and Peter. Another twenty-two people were taken prisoner, then tortured and killed in Srebrenica camps. When their bodies were returned, they had been mutilated.

"'Tell your readers about that!' Ratko said."

Milan said Ratko had explained how the Bosnian Government was pushing for safe havens in the area, but that the towns they wanted UN peacekeepers to turn into safe havens were all historically Serbian towns: Srebrenica, Goražde, Žepa. Orić and his colleagues wanted to use them as cover where Bosnian Serbs could not go, but Bosnian Muslim militia could use as bases to fire rockets from.

Milan said that Ratko and Mick had had a spat about the killings of JNA men in Sarajevo – the incident over which Goran and Ana had clashed some months earlier. Mladić had repeated the claim that forty-two men had been ambushed and killed in Dobrovoljačka Street. Mick said that he had been in a side street nearby with media colleagues and, while the ambush was real, the number of fatalities was closer to six.

Milan said he had been surprised by how calmly Mladić had taken Mick's claim after their initial clash. "He said to Mick, almost as if he was sad rather than angry, 'It was the darkest day in recent times for the Serbian nation, and now the Western media wants to write even that piece of history out of the record books.' And he shook his head."

Milan said that the interview had pretty much wound up when Mick had asked how the Bosnian Serb Army might respond in the event of UN peacekeepers being replaced by armed NATO troops and/or warplanes. "Ratko said that maybe some foreign powers would like to conduct military intervention, but he said, 'I want to remind them that they can come to Bosnia and Hercegovina but the question is "How will they leave?" This kind of adventure will create a black hole in which many will disappear.'"

Milan said that at that point Mick asked the question that prompted the international headlines. He described Ratko's quip that "one furious Serb can do a lot of damage with just one match", and his hint that London or Washington might be at risk from a worldwide Serbian diaspora, as "probably open-goal invitations from Mick that Ratko felt he couldn't miss". Milan said he and Ratko hadn't realised at the time the potential power of the comments. "I'm not even sure Mick did until he got back to his hotel and thought it all through. Then, next day – boom!" Milan mimicked an explosion with his hands.

"So how did Ratko take it?" asked Goran. "Was he mad at first?"

"No, he wasn't. We were both a bit shocked. To be honest, they were daft little threats. Not even Mick will have thought they were real. But when Ratko saw the headlines, well, he had a big grin on his face. When he read the whole piece, he was a bit annoyed that the story of Naser Orić hadn't featured higher up. I called Mick and I mentioned that, and he said he had included a reference to Orić and his atrocities. 'Yes,' I said, 'but not until paragraph twenty-five!'"

Milan said that Ratko had also liked the fact that *The Times*' man had referred to him as a man who'd read the classics of Tolstoy and Dostoyevsky. "He said to me, 'How the hell did he know that?' And I said, 'I told him.' I didn't tell him that you told me!

"Anyway, I got a bit of a gold star for the whole thing. Only thing is, Ratko's now expecting me to pull off more PR coups. A bit difficult when the only one I've managed was a complete fluke!" And Milan laughed.

Goran felt the glow of satisfaction shining from Milan at that moment but, after they left Goran's flat and went to a local bar, he was quickly back onto the flank of the ledge he was tiptoeing marked 'anxiety'. How might it end? How might Bosnia and Serbia extricate themselves from this conflict, Goran had asked?

"Well, I'm hoping that guy we met, David Owen, might come up with a peace plan. He's working with a guy called Vance. Former US Secretary of State. They might come up with something."

Goran risked a further personal question. "Generally, Milan, how are you finding it? It must be wearing."

Goran saw Milan take on a reflective air, as if he were examining the word 'wearing' in the round.

"'Wearing' doesn't quite capture it. To be honest, Goran, my nerves feel shredded. I might be largely office-bound but I can't get used to the scale of the violence. On both sides. I didn't know human beings could do such things to each other. I'm a quiet kid from Belgrade. How did I end up on the fringes of the siege of Sarajevo?" He paused and then breathed in. "I'm just trying to keep busy and get through each week. If it could end tomorrow, no one would be happier than me. But it won't – so I'll just keep my head down." He forced a smile. "And keep spinning for Ratko!"

7

It was two years into the conflicts that were breaking up Yugoslavia and already there had been tens of thousands of combatant and innocent civilian victims. They were watching TV, and Goran was laying a hand gently on the back of Ana's hand. He felt he could make the observation without breaching their unspoken rule of leaving political developments unadorned with commentary or analysis.

"You know this could be the end of it all, Ana?"

The preparations that Milan had hoped were being worked up by David Owen and Cyrus Vance had now crystallised into a fully fledged peace plan: the VOPP; the Vance-Owen Peace Plan. Now it was being hawked around the Balkans, from Croatia to Bosnia, Serbia to Montenegro.

"Do you really think so?" replied Ana. Goran felt he detected hope rather than optimism in her voice.

"Yes, I do," said Goran. "I don't know whether it's a long-term solution but it sounds to me as if outside pressure to get something signed and stop the killing is building up. I think even Slobo is backing it."

Goran had heard that Serbian President Slobodan Milošević was tiring of the trade and financial sanctions that the UN Security Council had imposed on Serbia one year earlier. And, although the Miloševićs and Mladićs and others at the top of the tree were cushioned from the shortages that affected most ordinary families, rampant inflation and the glumness of the general populace was making running Serbia challenging to say the least. Milošević wanted an end to sanctions, and he was reportedly putting pressure on the Bosnian Serbs to sign up to the VOPP.

A sharp thrill shot through Goran as he considered the effect a deal could have on Ana. All the tension, all the suppressed anxiety that she was bottling up and refusing to talk about could be banished, if not in a moment, then certainly at the end of what should be a finite process. And if, counter-intuitively, their love had grown deeper during this period of discussion paralysis, Goran was confident that its profundity would remain once the wars were over. Why might it not? Ratko wouldn't be removed from his orbit, and the possibility for which Goran had shamefully hoped – of his being killed in action – would be gone, but on balance an end to the conflicts and the killing had to be preferable to the current situation. The higher her father's profile, the more loudly he was lauded by Serb nationalists as a hero, the more Goran sensed Ana shrunk inside herself. Once the wars were over, he could begin the process of trying to wean her away from her father. Yes – it was as explicit as that. He couldn't bear to split with her, but he was facing up to the challenge. He *would* take it on. He had to believe that he could persuade her to choose him above her murderous, perhaps even genocidal father. An image of her just months ago, hugging her father and his beaming back at her, shot into Goran's mind, as if his subconscious were warning him that the battle would be no pushover. Yes, he was a long way from being in a position to articulate his arguments to her, but it was a duty that he had to shoulder even if, at its most extreme, it could make or break his life.

Across the former Yugoslavia, people became experts in the canton system, as Owen and Vance sought to package Bosnia into ten separate, Swiss-style pockets – an attempt to prevent the partition of Bosnia and halt Croatian and Serbian plans to carve the heart out of it. Goran watched nervously as Owen and Vance ticked off the signatories: the deal was seen as good for the Croats; Bosnia's President Izetbegović was persuaded; pressure from Milošević appeared to have won the Bosnian Serb leader Karadžić's begrudging backing – though, in a typical sleight of hand designed to avoid being blamed if the deal went bad, he insisted on a caveat that meant his signature had to be endorsed by a vote of the Bosnian Serb Assembly. The Assembly vote would be the last piece in the VOPP jigsaw.

Goran watched the proceedings live on TV from his own student flat. He had felt it unwise to follow the debate with Ana by his side. It would have been like watching a televised football match and not being allowed to shout from the sofa.

Unusually, and with dubious constitutional propriety, despite being the head of another state, President Milošević had succeeded in landing an invitation not just to attend the session but also to address the Bosnian Serb representatives. Never much of an orator, Milošević told the gathering, "A decision in favour of peace is in the interest of the Bosnian Serbs and the entire Serbian nation." Goran had followed the politics sufficiently closely to know that a threat of NATO bombing of Bosnian Serb and perhaps Serb targets lay behind his comments – unarticulated, inexplicit.

Goran's sense from the proceedings was that the debate was drifting towards a 'yes' vote that would rubber-stamp VOPP as the vehicle to lead Serbia, Croatia and Bosnia out of strife. Goran wasn't sure it would mean a laying down of arms – there were guns everywhere in the Balkans – but it should mean an end to much of the killing and a drift towards some kind of normality, even if it was hard to remember these days what normality had felt like.

But unexpectedly, the session chairman, Momčilo Krajišnik – close to Karadžić and believed to be a VOPP sceptic – decided to postpone the end of the debate and the vote until after a ceremonial dinner. After the dinner, the debate resumed and, even from the armchair in his Belgrade flat, Goran could sense that the momentum driving the Assembly to a 'yes' vote had been stalled.

And then the commander-in-chief of the Bosnian Serb Army, with a bulging file of documents under his arm, was striding towards the speaker's podium. Goran tensed. If it came to a choice, Goran knew Ratko would favour continued conflict. He had his hands on seventy per cent of Bosnian territory and he was unlikely to be wild about giving any of it up. He had been a professional soldier all his working life and now he was engaged in active soldiering. It wasn't every day a military leader came up against a war to fight – but he had one. In territorial terms, since 1991 he had been enormously successful. In reputational terms, he was at the peak of his powers.

At the podium, Ratko delivered a line that Goran had heard at the lunch table at the Mladić home: history was strewn with examples of Serbian military leaders and their armies having to put right poor decisions made by politicians. The Bosnian Serb Army had secured the protection of Bosnian Serb communities, and now politicians were planning on throwing much of that away. He called for the technical staff in the chamber to flash up on screen the charts he had prepared. Charts? What were these? The first chart showed the Bosnian territory currently occupied by his army. The second showed the demographic distribution of Bosnian Serbs. His killer slide superimposed the outlines of the proposed VOPP settlement upon his first two slides. The graphic showed not just a significant reduction in Serb-held territory if the peace plan were accepted; it showed also vulnerable isolation for whole sections of the Bosnian Serb population.

"Colleagues, are you seriously asking me to accept this? To leave our people so vulnerable? After all they've suffered at the hands of the Turks?" And looking pointedly at Milošević, he said, "Some of you have suggested between the lines of your fine speeches that, if we don't sign up to this, there will be Western intervention. That they'll rain bombs down on us from the sky. Well, let me tell you: my men are not afraid of Western intervention."

And he strode from the podium. The vote was lost; a referendum of the Bosnian Serb people on VOPP was called. Every onlooker knew that the result of that would be a resounding 'no', and that the peace plan would be dead. Milošević, unused to having to deal with the vulgarities of a vote that hadn't been rigged for him in advance, had been outmanoeuvred. A rare occurrence. On the TV footage, his mouth appeared to be popping like a goldfish's, with no words coming out.

Later it would emerge that, as Milošević scuttled off, escaping the Assembly through a side door, Mladić had crowed to his entourage, "It's fantastic – just like Real Madrid's best days!" Football-crazy Bosnian Serbs would have appreciated the comparison.

Goran understood that, if Mladić's short tour de force wasn't the only factor, it was a significant element in the killing of the VOPP. Politicians, diplomats and leaders had dragged the peace plan to within an inch of endorsement. Ratko had kicked it into the long grass. What Goran couldn't know then was that, by mortally wounding the VOPP, Mladić was creating the space for more than two years of additional conflict and tens of thousands of further killings.

When he met Ana at the faculty the following day, Goran said nothing about the Assembly session, her father's contribution, and the vote to put the VOPP to a referendum of the people – equivalent to a death warrant for the process. She gave no indication of any knowledge of the proceedings. But, as Goran resumed their pact of silence, he felt a profound sorrow.

Where will this all end? he asked himself.

8

Goran could sense the tension in Ana releasing almost as soon as the aeroplane left the tarmac and set off on its journey to Moscow. Goran had feared that the optimistic, altruistic spirit that he had found so attractive when they'd first met was being inexorably dragged down, and he had wondered how long it might be before she was under water. But as the aeroplane put more and more miles between itself and the former Yugoslavia, it was as if Ana was able gradually to shut out the war from her mind, forget how conflicted she felt, and look to a future in which she could devote herself to a caring profession.

Goran, Ana and some other students from their medical faculty were flying to Moscow for an international conference of medical students around the theme of *The Future of Medicine: How to Heal the Developing World*. Goran sensed that Ana saw it as a few days in which she could move off her hinterland and mingle with peers from around the world, peers who would be blissfully unaware of her connections and her blameless association with notoriety. She lifted the armrest separating her from him, leaned against his shoulder, slid her left arm inside his right, interlocked their fingers and squeezed. He could feel her thrill.

Goran liked Moscow. He had visited twice before and he loved its scale and its majesty, but he loved too its wickedness and its glaring architectural mash-ups. The early-sixteenth-century Novodevichy Convent with its five-domed cathedral and high bell tower, replete with frescoes, was one of his favourites. And then there were the hideous grey-brown concrete Soviet-era apartment blocks. Each city had its sublime and its ridiculous. Here the gap was a chasm.

"I could never live there, Ana. It's brash and there's always a hint of menace in the air, but there's something thrilling about it too. You feel as if it's life on the edge. It's scary but, as soon as you leave, you feel you need to go back."

And he told Ana a story that at first seemed trivial but, on reflection, was a cartoon sketch that captured the broader tapestry of Moscow life. He had been in a city centre bar, thick with cigarette smoke, the level of chatter near deafening, when a customer had complained that he had been short-changed. Rather than apologise and hand back the missing roubles, the barman had stood on a crate behind the beer pumps, leaned over and slapped the complainant in the face with an open palm. The message was, *Don't come in here and expect not to be ripped off, and when you are, don't expect the people in charge to look out for you.*

Goran chuckled at the memory. Ana smiled too.

But since he had last visited, the Berlin Wall had fallen, a hard-line Communist coup had failed, President Gorbachev had stood aside for Boris Yeltsin, the Soviet Union was no more, and Russia was once again an independent state. What kind of chaos would characterise Moscow now, two years on?

At Vnukovo Airport, the medical students were met by a woman with a placard who directed them to buses that would scoop up visitors from planes from around the world and take them to their accommodation on the Moscow State University campus.

Just south of a kink in the Moskva River, ten kilometres from the city centre, the front prospect of the Lomonosov university building hoves into view, an unapologetically huge monument to the Soviet education system and an unambiguous statement of the privileged space reserved for learning in Russian society. If its facade spoke of too many learning spaces to count, its wedding-cake tiers, the red star at its pinnacle dramatically reaching to the sky, its colonnaded entrance, its ornate clock faces, and its classical, figurative sculptures all combined to differentiate it from any hotel with inflated pretensions. It had a grandeur that briefly took Goran's breath away and added to his sense that the days ahead could be special; his sense that Ana was continuing to thaw by his side and might be able to enjoy the conference added to his optimism.

But if the exterior of the University was impressive, after Goran and Ana had left their student accommodation for the conference reception inside the main building they found the interior to be still more breathtaking; an apogee of design: no expense spared on now priceless marble of bold and subtle colours and shades, on ornate stonework, and on daringly integrated columns and arches.

In their room beforehand, Ana had been quiet but, Goran sensed, silently exhilarated. Just as he was beginning to think that it couldn't be possible for one person to spend so much time getting ready, she had emerged from the bathroom, looking ravishing. Her hair, cut in his preferred elf-like style, was shiny; she was wearing bright red glossy lipstick, a tight red thigh-length dress, and shiny black stilettoes.

As he leaned in to kiss her, she laid a forefinger on his lips. "No touching," she said with a mock firmness, anxious that he didn't smudge her lipstick and force her to reapply. "Well, not yet anyway," she added.

"Ooh! Minx!" Goran said with a smile. He was glowing inside at this vision of beauty, this tease.

As they made their way through reception and upstairs to the first floor, pillars of milky blue mottled marble, topped with finely worked bronze fittings, flanked the staircase; maroon-and-violet marble lampstands between each pair of pillars. A chandelier sparkled above the top of the stair. Light flooded in through the first-floor windows on either side of the staircase. It was too beautiful to pass comment on. It forbade banalities. In an open area laid with a red, plush carpet and ringed with ribbed, classical marble pillars, etchings of the profiles of some of the University's founding fathers and the world's greatest scientists looked down from a raised border around the room. Students were gathering.

Ana and Goran picked up a glass of champagne each, as they entered the space. As he took his first sip and the dry metallic notes acted like a jump-start to his taste buds, he considered the rarefied environment and the lavish surroundings that they had stepped into and he realised that he felt privileged, respected and welcome here. These were feelings that had been central to much of his life. Not a day had gone by when he had not been grateful for the gifts he had been given, the family he had been born into, and the warmth and reassurance that had surrounded him. How shocking to realise two thousand kilometres from Belgrade that his life had been devoid of those elements for around two years now. It had hardly spiralled down, but the conflicts and their impact on Ana were conspiring to drag him down and strip him of his natural optimism. He wouldn't let them, he vowed to himself.

Photos and short pen portraits of those attending were displayed on easels on either side of the entrance to the reception space. Delegates gathered around them, to locate their own names and to absorb the conference's global reach, before moving into the main body of the room. Goran estimated that there were around two hundred invitees. The reception space was already populated with around 150 people and more were arriving all the time. The UK, France, Belgium, Germany, Australia, Egypt and Saudi Arabia were among the countries represented, according to the attendance list.

Goran's preoccupation, since he had driven over the border with Bulgaria to Sofia and then taken their flight to Moscow, had been Ana's well-being. It was only now, as he began to imbibe the sense of excitement rippling through this roomful of chattering, bright-eyed, ambitious young people, that he felt able to relax a little himself, to begin to enjoy the fact that he had been allowed to make this trip, and to set aside some of his concerns for his girlfriend. For the first time since the trip and the conference had stopped being concepts located in the relatively remote future and had become exercises in logistics, he was able unequivocally to look forward to the event and to the spark he expected to receive from the medical experts who would lead it and the fellow students with whom he would share the experience.

Goran and Ana caught up with some of their friends from the Belgrade Medical School and, through them, were introduced to other students: some from Serbia; others from France and the UK. It was all very convivial.

After a while, Goran noticed one of the delegates about ten metres away looking frequently in their direction. He began to feel some slight concerns, because the student's interest lay clearly in Ana and Goran suspected that he might try to hit on her before the night was out. Although he found wearisome the prospect of having to be involved in keeping the potential suitor at arm's length, perhaps there was something of a subliminal fear of real competition too, because there could be no doubt: this was an extraordinarily beautiful man. Standing around six feet seven inches tall, he towered above the rest of the delegates. He had the long, straight nose of someone of noble birth, huge brown eyes, high cheekbones, slightly hollowed-out cheeks, and a jawbone cut in a strong V-shape. Not even a wispy beard and a fluffy upper lip could detract from his good looks, though it was bizarre that, in this roomful of youngsters in fashionable dress, he had topped off his navy-blue pinstriped suit and white open-necked shirt with a light brown woollen *pakol*. It was a hat that he would never be seen without throughout the conference, and it represented an audacious – and some would say provocative – religious and political statement, given that it was the headgear of choice of the Afghan mujahideen.

Soviet President Leonid Brezhnev's catastrophic invasion of Afghanistan in 1979 had led to seven and a half years of war, international opprobrium, nearly fifteen thousand Soviet deaths, over fifty thousand wounded, and over four hundred thousand troops ravaged by typhoid, hepatitis and other infectious diseases. It had become known as the Soviet Union's Vietnam, and some even credited it as one of the causes of the downfall of the Soviet Union itself.

While the bearer of such headgear might just about get away with it at a specialist international conference on a private site ten kilometres out of town, Goran suspected that he would be foolhardy, or have a death wish, were he to venture into the streets of central Moscow wearing his *pakol*, however controversial a figure he wanted to cut.

"Prick!" Goran muttered to himself.

Eventually, the man made his move, picking a path between champagne-swilling delegates, nursing a glass of orange juice. Goran stuck close to Ana so that he couldn't try to peel her off.

"Watch out for this wise guy," he warned Ana, suspecting that she had clocked him sometime earlier, given his frequent glances in her direction and his infuriatingly good looks.

He turned out to be Jacob, of Dutch Indonesian origin, studying at a medical faculty in The Hague. The Dutch blood explained his height; his Indonesian ancestry contributing to his glorious copper complexion and his noble features.

"Your badges say Yugoslavia. So, is it Yugoslavia – or the former Yugoslavia?"

It was a smart-arse question, but at least it was hardly a chat-up line, thought Goran, bridling.

"As you'll be aware, the region is in a state of… flux," said Goran. He wanted to say, *What's with the hat, goon?*, but he resisted the temptation.

Jacob was nodding. "A state of flux… y-e-e-e-s. And which part of this state of flux are you both from?" And he smiled, as if admiring his own laconic humour.

Ana piped in. "We're from Serbia. We're at the medical school in Belgrade."

"Serbia, eh? Well, there's some serious shit going on down there, isn't there?"

It was a question that barely deserved an answer, and both Goran and Ana made as if they were searching out acquaintants in other parts of the room.

Jacob persisted. "I mean, I hope you don't mind me saying, but from where the rest of the world is standing, it's the Serbs who've caused all of the conflict. Some of my Muslim brothers in Bosnia are really suffering."

So, that was it: he was Muslim, but almost certainly a recent convert and, Goran suspected, as much to impress his contemporaries with his radicalism as out of conviction.

Ana was already replying, though Goran wished she had not. "I think you'll find it was Croatia and Slovenia that broke up the Federation. Not Serbia," she said curtly. "But, if you don't mind, I'm here for a medical conference, not to talk about politics. It's a complex situation. It's difficult for outsiders to understand." She turned her shoulder to him, as if to indicate that the conversation was at an end.

Jacob was undaunted. "Oh, I think we *do* understand," he said. And, in a clear invasion of her personal space, he leaned over and fingered Ana's identity badge. "Ana Mladić," he said. "Now, don't I recognise that name from somewhere?"

Goran wrapped his arm around Ana's shoulder and eased her a foot or so away from Jacob. "Do you mind?" he said sharply, glaring at Jacob. The tension needle that he and Ana had been fighting to bring down risked breaking the meter dial again.

There was a loud sound of a hand tapping a microphone. The course leader was about to spare them from further scrutiny from Jacob. As the professor and his English interpreter began to welcome the delegates, Goran eased Ana through the crowd until they were safely removed from Jacob's orbit. Goran didn't look back to see whether he had continued to watch them.

The speeches finished, Goran and Ana recharged their glasses a couple of times, and Jacob did not try to attempt another round of inquisition. The champagne made Goran feel light-headed, though even the sense of euphoria it had conjured up wasn't quite enough to banish entirely the image of the six-foot-seven-inch man with the Afghan *pakol*.

They didn't mention Jacob as they made their way back to their accommodation. Once back in the room, Ana, a little tipsy but steady enough, gripped Goran's lapels, tugged him down towards her and said, "Now you can touch…"

And Goran did – comprehensively and at length.

The following day, Ana's outfit of a neat black twinset and white blouse showed that she was taking the conference deadly seriously. It was work, not recreation. Goran knew that she was hoping and expecting to mine it for as much information as she could, perhaps even taking steers from its experts that might help her choose the medical path she should first embark upon, once qualified.

The conference was to open with all delegates in one lecture hall before breaking out into themed groups later in the morning. The professor who had welcomed them the night before was outlining how the conference would be structured. As he began to wind up, Goran noticed Jacob on the other side of the lecture hall, near the front, thrusting his arm in the air as if wanting to speak. He thought he heard the words 'point of order' coming from the direction of Jacob.

As the professor wound to a close, he noticed Jacob, who was now bobbing up and down, and said, "Yes? Sir? Do you have a question?"

Jacob nodded.

"Take a microphone to him," said the professor.

When the microphone arrived, Jacob was immediately transformed.

Part actor, part preacher, he had seized an audience and he was going to milk it. "Professor, delegates. I have a point of order that it is important for all of us to consider before we get down to business." He clutched the microphone like someone accustomed to the stage, adding flourishes with his other arm, strutting as best he could in the limited space around him.

"I suspect we have all seen on our screens the tragic images of the bloody conflict now taking place in Bosnia. It is largely – but not uniquely – my Muslim brothers and sisters who are being driven from their homes, tortured, raped, murdered. These are scenes not witnessed in Europe since the Second World War."

"What the fucccck?!" Ana whispered. Goran sensed her tensing.

The professor cut in. "Sir, I'm not sure what your point of order or question is. We need to proceed."

"Sir." Jacob was holding the audience and not about to give it up. "My point of order and my question are these. One Bosnian Serb leader is primarily responsible for sanctioning the rape, the torture, the killing. That man is General Ratko Mladić. We have all seen him on our screens. He has blood on his hands. He is guilty not just of ethnic cleansing, but of genocide."

Despite the detail of the build-up, Goran was still unprepared for what would come next.

"My question to you, Professor, and to all delegates, is this: we have in our midst, at this conference, the daughter of General Mladić. Is it right that, as we gather here to find better outcomes for the world's underprivileged and repressed, the daughter of one of the world's most brutal killers should be allowed to remain among us? My point of order is that Ana Mladić, from Belgrade Medical Faculty, be barred from this conference and removed from the university campus."

Goran gasped. He felt Ana stir. She leapt to her feet. He tried to tug her down. Best to ignore this maniac. But the words were already out of her mouth in a scream across the lecture hall. She hadn't needed a microphone.

"You don't know what you're talking about! You're talking rubbish!" The words shattered the stunned silence.

Goran was aware of delegates around him looking on, open-mouthed.

And then Ana crumbled. "It's just not true…" she said, her voice softening, and then she folded into tears and sobbed.

Before Goran could stop her, she was bursting past the other delegates in their row and then rushing towards the exit at the back of the hall. Goran went to follow her but she had put significant space between them. As he made it out of the hall, he saw her disappear into a sanctuary he could not access: the women's toilets.

Goran would learn from faculty colleagues later that the professor leading the conference gave Jacob short shrift. This was not a political arena. It was a space for medical studies, and his allegations against people who were not present was inappropriate. Furthermore, he should apologise to the delegate to whom he had caused distress.

Still playing the actor and performing for the audience, Jacob had replied, "May Allah – *salla Allahu alayhi wa-sallam* – bless you nonetheless, Professor, for hearing my point of order, and *subḥānahu wa-taʿālā*: praise be to Him, the glorified and lofty."

A female delegate appeared at Goran's side and offered to go into the ladies' and try to calm Ana. A full fifteen minutes later, she emerged with Ana. Ana's tears had washed away her foundation. Her mascara, which had no doubt smudged across her face, had been inexpertly washed off, leaving tiny spider footsteps here and there. A couple of blotches had spilt onto her blouse.

Goran led her to a stone bench by the side of the hallway. "You okay?" he asked. It was a dumb question – but he didn't have one that was better.

"No, not really," she said. She was managing to keep at bay any further gagging or sobbing, but she was pale and wore what Goran, once he had found the right words, would describe in the retelling as an air of devastation. All the joy and the optimism she had accrued between Sofia and Moscow had just gone in an instant. She had tucked her horrific secret into a closet and Jacob had unlocked the door and chased it back out into the open in one brutal, shocking action.

One of their Belgrade friends appeared and explained that the professor had shot down Jacob. Ana should come back into the lecture hall.

"I'm not sure that I can go back in," said Ana, her eyes cast down.

"Ana, come on," Goran pleaded. "We're not going to let that big shot ruin this for us. We're not."

Eventually, Ana gave way. "Okay, okay," she said.

As they made for the door, Goran said, "Anyway, he's not a proper Muslim. He's a plastic Muslim. He's a disgrace to Islam." He wasn't sure why he had said it or whether it would soothe Ana in any way. He felt slightly better for pushing the thought out, though.

As Ana and Goran and their colleague from Belgrade went back into the lecture hall, around a quarter of the delegates, their curiosity getting the better of their good manners, turned to see this humiliated young woman walk back in. What would they be thinking, Goran wondered? Most would be thinking, *Poor woman*, he sensed, but there may be some fascinated by their first sight of the daughter of a murderous, internationally renowned criminal.

Jacob kept his distance throughout the day, resisting the invitation from the professor to apologise to the delegate he had wronged. And Goran knew that, had he made an attempt to come over and say sorry, he would have blocked him from approaching. Yes – all six feet seven of him.

Back in their room that night, Ana sat on a wooden chair, resisting the softer embrace of an armchair, as if ascetically punishing herself for finding herself in this situation. Goran could feel the charge coming his way.

Eventually she spoke. "Goran, why didn't you defend me? Why didn't you stand up and say, 'It's not true'?"

Goran crouched down before her, took one of her forefingers in his hand and said softly, "Ana, which bit should I have said wasn't true?" There. He had said it.

Ana began to cry softly again. "I don't know," she said, her words distorted by tears. "You should have just stepped in."

Goran knew that she had been up and firing back at Jacob before he could have responded, but now was not the time to argue over the choreography of those moments. But his own words to Ana were now resounding inside his head. He was coming to terms with the fact that he had just told her in as many words that, if Jacob's request was absurd, not one of his allegations was untrue.

Later that night, after the sweet communion of twenty-four hours earlier, she lay in the bed with her back to him, though, in the forthcoming days, he would sense that she needed him more than ever. She would cling to him, hold his hand, be needy, ask to be hugged – but there was now between them a new, invisible barrier. They might never be quite so close to one another again as they were when they had arrived in Moscow. But if he hated Jacob and would never forgive him for seeking a stage for his moment of celebrity, when Goran weighed up how he and Ana had ended up in this realigned relationship, he knew that Jacob had simply been a catalyst. Without him, another catalyst would have come along and the same crisis point and consequence would have been reached.

Slowly, gradually, it dawned on Goran what it was he had to do. He would cling to his Ana and never let her go, despite that slight cooling of their ardour. He would make it a temporary aberration. He would claim her back in her entirety. He would break down that invisible barrier and recreate a bond incapable of being dissolved; one that would see them through a long, happy life together.

Yes, he knew what he had to do. He had to make Ana face up to the reality of her father's actions. She had to renounce him to free herself. And renouncing Ratko would bind them, Goran and Ana, together forever. But how might he do it? And when should he do it? He suspected that, when the time was right, he would know it.

9

For some reason Goran was eager to tell Milan about the episode in Moscow, so he was relieved when Milan called him by chance around ten days after they had returned to Belgrade.

In those ten days, Goran had become aware of how quickly the story of Jacob and Ana had swept through the medical faculty. He didn't know which of their colleagues had begun to spread the story and he didn't really blame anyone for failing to resist the temptation of sharing it with friends and colleagues, but he was aware of more than several of their fellow students looking at Ana in a slightly different way, and he imagined that Ana had noticed it too.

If close friends felt – and some even expressed – sympathy for her, Goran felt that much of the attention had a ghoulish aspect to it, and when they were moving through crowded areas on the campus, he made sure to put his arm around her shoulder, as if to say, *If you have an issue with Ana because of what happened in Moscow, you have one with me too.* She was in the same family situation as she had been in before she'd flown to Moscow, so there was no cause to view her differently. And he felt no contradiction between his protective feelings and actions now and his intention to alter that Mladić family dynamic sometime in the future. He would try to rescue her from it, not abandon her to it.

Goran needed several degrees of internal inquisition to understand why it was important to tell the story to Milan. He dismissed quickly the idea that he wanted someone in Mladić's entourage to feel ashamed about the scale of notoriety that was now rippling out internationally. Ratko's team had actively celebrated that following his 'just one match' quip.

Goran had to admit in the end that there was something about his recounting the detail and the drama of the incidents that gave him a lift that might at first have seemed unlikely. The challenge he faced had been encapsulated in their two skirmishes with Jacob, in Ana's fleeing the lecture hall in tears, and in his own harrowing question to her about Jacob's allegations: "Which bit should I have said wasn't true?" Yes, that was it. Every powerful story was a thrill to retell, but this story also laid bare the scale of the challenge he faced.

He didn't want to share with Milan just yet his intention to persuade Ana to disown her father. It would be unfair to share that secret with him at this stage. In fact, it might burden him unreasonably, given his working relationship with Ratko. But Milan had just the right degree of proximity to and remoteness from Goran to make him the right person to share this with. He wasn't a bosom buddy who would proceed to ask personal questions that might flush out Goran's longer-term intentions, but he was a sensitive soul, a literary man who would instantly grasp the drama of the story. Goran guessed he would be shocked but thrilled by it. His imagination did take over for a moment as he visualised Milan jotting the details down in a pocketbook – a pocketbook in which he logged episodes that he might be able to recycle in his own fiction somewhere down the line.

As he reflected further, Goran acknowledged too that he sensed that Milan might be able to share his trauma. He was attempting less to tell Milan that his boss was a monster; more to say to him, *This is my pain. Do you understand that?*

From Milan's comments after he had listened to the story, Goran sensed that, if he had not hit bullseye, he was pretty close to double top.

"Oh, wow, Goran! That must've been so tough… for Ana; for you…" Milan paused, and Goran sensed that he was loving the colour, the detail. "And so he really wore that *pakol* and pinstriped suit for the whole conference?"

"He did, Milan. I just wished we had had time to take a coach trip to Red Square. I'd love to have seen him wear his hat there!"

And they both laughed. Then Goran realised he hadn't spoken to Milan since Ratko's role in torpedoing the Vance-Owen Peace Plan.

"I wasn't there," Milan said. "And he didn't ask me for advice on how to pitch it, but I heard about it afterwards."

"The debate was slipping away before he put his slides up," said Goran. "But those slides – well, they just about killed it dead."

"You know me," said Milan. "I don't go in for much of that Greater Serbia bollocks, but what you need to remember – and this was what Ratko was trying to say in the Assembly – is that many of those Serbian villages and settlements in Bosnia, their families have lived there for centuries. They're not interlopers or refugees. Those really are their homes."

"I know, Milan. But that's always been the beauty of Bosnia, hasn't it? People of different origins and ethnicities and religions living side by side… tolerantly. It's only since a couple of years ago that Milošević and his gang decided that, in order to protect those Bosnian Serbs, we had to beat up Croats and shoot Bosnian Muslims." Goran paused. "But, hell, let's not go there. What happens next? Now the VOPP's dead, does it get worse before it gets better?"

Milan explained that the situation was delicately balanced. Ratko was part convinced that a ceasefire might be timely. Without the peace plan, perhaps he could freeze in place his seventy per cent occupation of Bosnia. That might be a good outcome, because it appeared that the Bosnian Muslims had not just turned much of their manufacturing capability to weapons production; they also seemed to have found ways of breaching the arms embargo, and the intelligence was that weaponry and ammunition were being smuggled into Bosnia from sources ranging from Iran and Saudi Arabi to various Muslim groups based in Africa. "They're showing better fighting skills and organisation too, so a ceasefire might be timely, as we're stretched trying to defend so much Bosnian territory."

But Milan said that, while Ratko was partially attracted to a ceasefire, he didn't believe he would sign up to that until he had cleaned up more towns along the Bosnian border with Serbia. "Do you remember me telling you about his interview with Mick from *The Times*? He's obsessed with sorting out those guys shooting at us from the likes of Srebrenica," said Milan. "So there, it might get worse before it gets better."

Goran was troubled both by the news of an emboldened Bosnian Army chipping back at Mladić's men, and by Milan's sense that there was unfinished business along Bosnia's eastern border with Serbia. Neither sounded like fertile ground for a ceasefire. "Oh well, Milan. I'll not be visiting Pale or Sarajevo any time soon, but do let me know if you're back on leave in Belgrade any time."

"I will, I will, Goran. And sorry about your little difficulty in Moscow. I hope Ana feels better about it before long."

They ended the call. Goran felt glad he had shared the drama of the last fortnight with Milan. He had felt the empathy that he had hoped to tease out of Milan, even if it barely altered the situation he found himself in by one jot.

10

As the months ticked by with no obvious new routes to resolution, Goran and Ana threw themselves into their medical studies. There was so much to learn and Goran found he could forget the conflicts temporarily in his moments of deepest immersion. He doubted that Ana could lose herself as effectively, but because she stuck so rigidly to her oath of silence on all matters relating to the conflicts, he couldn't know for certain.

As 1993 tipped into 1994 and it would soon be three years since the conflicts had broken out, they had found some succour in their habit of studying quietly alongside one another in Ana's flat. They could go for long periods without speaking to one another, yet Goran felt without fear of contradiction that their shared space and endeavour was mutually strengthening.

It was early February and, after an extended and successful study session, Goran had turned on the TV to catch the news. Sometimes Ana would remonstrate and say, "Oh, Goran – do we really need to have that stuff on?", as if keeping the TV shut down might alter the reality out there across the Balkans. On this occasion, before Ana could express a view, the distress of the TV reporter was evident.

"I can only describe the carnage," she said. "Many of the images are too distressing for us to broadcast."

It emerged that a 120-millimetre shell had been lobbed into the popular Markale marketplace in the centre of Sarajevo shortly after noon. Surrounded by seven- and eight-storey buildings, the market had felt like a relatively safe space, the reporter explained, as civilians shopped for fruit and vegetables or brought items for barter.

"There were literally hundreds of people gathered here when the shell hit. Initial estimates put the death toll at over fifty with over one hundred more injured – many of the survivors, it would appear, with life-changing injuries."

The reporter went on to describe, as delicately as she could, the scale of the terror. Individuals decapitated, limbs strewn among the scattered and pulped produce, blood pooling underfoot. "By the time I arrived on the scene, fifteen minutes after the blast, ordinary civilians were lifting the wounded onto makeshift stretchers: sheets of metal, wooden panels – anything that could carry victims to a car or a van that would take them to a hospital or a morgue. Mothers, grandmothers were still wailing by the side of the market, but overall, there was an atmosphere of stunned silence. In a city that has seen outrage after outrage, not even the battered civilians of Sarajevo could have imagined such an act of terror; such a scene of devastation."

Goran could feel his blood beginning to boil within him. He gritted his teeth to try to hold down his rage, but what images the reporter felt able to share with viewers were just too much. It felt as if a valve had blown within him, and he heard himself scream at the television set. "I'm a Serbian, and a proud Serbian, and no one – *no one* – does *that* in my name!" He didn't make eye contact with Ana, but he sensed her alarm. He grabbed his jacket and stormed out of her flat, down the stairs, and into the chilly air. He buttoned his coat and trivially wished he had picked up his hat too. He was muttering and fuming still. "Bastards! Bastards!"

Goran had no doubt, given the pattern of events that had characterised the siege so far, that this had been a Bosnian Serb shell.

Milan had told him how the Bosnian Muslims regularly tried to provoke the Bosnian Serb Army in Sarajevo. "We'll agree a ceasefire in a district and then they'll snipe at us from a school or a hospital. Then, when we fire back, they accuse us of breaching the ceasefire and firing at schoolchildren and the sick. They're no angels, I can tell you," he had said.

But Goran swept the thought aside. There were Bosnian Serb fingerprints all over this episode, he believed, and this was one outrage way, way too far.

He didn't know where he was going, but at every corner he turned in the streets near Ana's flat, the dome of the Temple of St Sava that had been raised less than five years earlier demanded attention. Goran wasn't a believer but he knew that a project decades in the planning and construction would soon see one of the finest churches in Christendom dominate the skyline of his own neighbourhood. For Goran, in that moment, the persistence and ambition of the men who had striven to emulate or outstrip the architects of the finest churches in Moscow and Istanbul simply to worship their God contrasted sharply with the actions of those who spoke grandly of a 'Greater Serbia', as if it were some sacred concept. These were people sufficiently tawdry of spirit to hurl shells at hundreds of innocent civilians going about their business in one of the most cosmopolitan capitals of Europe. If they weren't personally responsible for the deed, they were responsible for creating the environment that made the action 'permissible', insofar as it ever could be.

If his fury was abating, it did so in slow motion. He was angry at Milošević, though he didn't believe Markale had been his initiative. He was angry at Ratko, whose initiative it could conceivably have been. And, yes, hand on heart, he had to admit it: this time he was angry at Ana as well. There – he had said it. She was blameless, but through bloodline she had 'association'. And he couldn't tolerate that for much longer.

He thought of dropping by Čolak Antina. He knew his parents would be feeling as low as him at the news – but he wasn't in the mood for company. He would ask Milan one time to introduce him to his journalist father. What might *Borba* be writing about the atrocity at this very moment? He would like to talk things through with Mr Tešević at some point, though of course not now.

So Goran did what he frequently did when he was reflective or blue, or sometimes when he was full of the joys of life: he wandered through the streets of Belgrade, past Republic Square, up to Kalemegdan where old men played chess on tables set up along the paths through the park, and he kept on until he saw the wide stretch of the River Sava and then finally reached the point at which the Sava met the Danube.

As a child he had marvelled at the scale of the Danube. How could a river be so wide? And, if it were clean, might he one day be able to swim that far – from riverbank to riverbank? He had only seen it as far afield as

Vukovar in north-east Croatia and Novi Sad, and even then he had been thrilled to learn that it was the same river that flowed through Belgrade. But his father had explained that the Belgrade stretch was only halfway along a river that started in Germany's Black Forest and flowed nearly three thousand kilometres to a delta on the Black Sea.

This confluence of the Danube and the Sava gave him perspective. It located him. The first time he had ever been able to make sense of a map had been when he had drunk in this view and then identified it on the map. Maps did speak truth after all.

The wind off the rivers had an icy edge. The pale grey clouds carried no rain but Goran felt that snow might not be far away. Once he had breathed in until the cold had sunk into his lungs, he felt a degree of calmness descend upon him. His journey to this point had served its purpose. And he began to feel slightly ashamed of his anger towards Ana. Poor, blameless Ana. That anger towards her had been dislodged by the more typical love-ache in the pit of his stomach. He recalled the alarm he had sensed flushing through her as he had screamed at the TV. And if he didn't quite regret his scream, he regretted alarming her.

The light was about to fade fast. He felt calm enough to begin to wend his way back to Ana's flat. He would need to return there not just because his books were there, but to make it clear that he was not blaming her by staying away. He expected that the longer he stayed out, the more worried she might be.

He let himself into the flat. Ana looked across at him. He raised his eyebrows in silent acknowledgement.

"Hi," she said in a whisper.

Goran sat down in an armchair. He still said nothing, though he hoped Ana sensed that he was becalmed.

She came behind the chair and stood by its right arm. She laid her left hand on his right collarbone and rubbed it gently. "They're saying it's not clear which side fired the shell," she said quietly. "They say from the shell crater they can't be definitive."

"Oh, really?" Goran said neutrally. He looked up and into her eyes as he spoke, so she could see that, if he was still sad, he wasn't angry.

Reports later that evening suggested that sixty-eight people had been killed and 144 wounded by shrapnel from a mortar. It was being ranked as among the worst atrocities of the conflicts so far.

Ana had been right: initial analysis was that the mortar had flown in from a north-north-east direction. UN artillery specialists would ultimately conclude that the shell could have come from anywhere in a cone of two and a half square kilometres north-north-east of the marketplace – an area that straddled the confrontation line between Bosnian Muslim and Bosnian Serb forces, from a slice of land that encompassed the Bosnian Serb mortar position of Mrkovići, but which also contained some Bosnian Army positions.

The US was quick to lay the blame at the door of the Bosnian Serbs, Goran could not bring himself to believe that Bosnian Muslims would have shelled their own people in an attempt to bring down fresh international outrage upon the Bosnian Serbs, and Ana kept her own counsel.

But Goran sensed that one thing had shifted invisibly: he felt that Ana had felt his rage and she now realised that something in their situation had to change. Goran realised that he would have to marshal all his eloquence, deploy the keenest logic, but above all, convince her of his deepest love, if he was to help bring about the right kind of change.

11

For Goran, terms such as 'systemic thromboembolism' had a special ring to them. Had the echoing, colliding vowels within their tight consonant packaging been put together by poets rather than by clinicians? Sometimes it sounded so.

He revelled in these hours of quiet study: being tugged beneath the surface, swallowed up by the scientific concepts and proofs contained in the likes of *Robbins Basic Pathology*, Chapter 4, 'Hemodynamic Disorders, Thromboembolism, and Shock'. He had been pleased by his levels of concentration that evening, and if the occasional poetry of the medical terms risked lifting him from the scientific to the artistic, they added a gilt edge to the learning experience that he was delighted to accommodate.

But the phone was ringing, and the phone hardly ever rang at 9pm on a Tuesday evening. If his initial reaction was irritation and resentment at having his concentration broken, relief followed hard on its heels. It would be Ana, changing her mind about their spending the night apart in their separate flats. She was calling him to come over and share her bed. He felt a warm flush – but then a jag of recollection. She had kissed him before they had gone their separate ways, as if to say that no grudges should be borne, but they had parted coolly.

Goran picked up the receiver before it could ring out. It wasn't Ana. It was her brother, Darko. Darko never rang him.

"Hi, Goran. It's Darko here. Er…"

Goran was somewhat taken aback by the fact that it was Darko, and Darko appeared set to embark upon a conversation that wasn't his normal style and wasn't something he felt particularly comfortable with.

"I'm just ringing about Ana," said Darko.

"Oh – does she want me to go over?"

"No... I mean, I don't know. I just wondered if you knew whether there was something up with her. She's just gone back to her flat now, but she seemed a bit upset about something."

"Did she say what?" Goran eased himself nervously from left foot to right and back again in a gentle rocking motion. Although this was a nervous reaction that would have been barely detectable even to someone alongside him in his flat, he was relieved that Darko couldn't see it. His mind flitted for a split second: *Robbins Basic Pathology*, Chapter 23, 'Central Nervous System'. The words 'subfalcine herniation' surfaced. Irrelevant to his situation, yet somehow comforting.

But Darko was explaining. "She came over – as usual. To see Dad. We played *Battleship*. As usual."

Goran raised his eyebrows in exasperation but gave Darko no verbal indication down the line of his irritation. It was one of the reasons he was pleased not to have accompanied Ana that night. Those bloody board games. So puerile, but so beloved of Ratko. Goran's sense was that they served two purposes for him: one, family bonding; and two, another chance to win at something. And he usually won. "Oh, yeah? Who won?" asked Goran.

"Ana won, actually." Darko managed a half-laugh.

"I bet your dad loved that," said Goran. Ratko was the most terrible loser, arguing rule infringements, conspiracy, or just plain cheating, whenever he lost.

"You can imagine," said Darko. He paused a moment before resuming. "It's just that Mum said I should ring you. Ana was behaving a bit strangely."

"Really? What do you mean?"

"Well, at times she appeared on the verge of tears. And at one point she said something we were all shocked by."

Goran stood stock-still. No rocking from foot to foot. He was expecting to be called to account. But Darko's tone was not accusatory.

"She said to my dad that she was thinking of quitting her medical degree."

"She said *what?!*" The idea came at Goran like a club.

"Yes. She said she was thinking of quitting school and going to the front line in Bosnia and working as a nurse. Caring for injured Bosnian Serb soldiers."

"Jeee-zuzz!" Goran had never had such a discussion with her. Where had this come from all of a sudden? "What did your dad say?"

"He told her not to be silly. He said, 'Come on, Ana – my girl's not a quitter, is she?' And he told her not to talk like that."

"So, did she say anything more about it?"

"No. She was still upset about something. Then, after the game was over, she said she had a headache, and she was going to go back to her flat." Darko said that their mother had tried to soothe her, asked her to stay the night at the family home, but she wouldn't. "I just wondered if she'd said anything to you. We were half-expecting you to come along tonight. Then, when she was behaving so strangely, we wondered if you two had had a bust-up."

Goran found it easy to adopt a reassuring tone. "No, no – nothing like that. It was just I had a bit of work to catch up on. So I couldn't come. But we're fine. Just fine. I'll give her a call and go over there, if she wants me to go across. I'm sure she'll be fine."

Darko seemed reassured by Goran's words and relieved to be able to get off the line. Goran's line hummed after Darko had hung up. He laid the receiver back on its cradle and stood motionless for a moment. A sense of shock was resonating within him. She had never told him that she might quit her degree – still less go to the front line in Bosnia. Not that he believed there was a real likelihood of either.

He resisted the temptation to call Ana straight away. He wanted to try to be clear in his mind as to what her state of mind might be before he made the call. And if he just made his way to her flat, might that not suggest that he was resiling from the ultimatum he had given? Might it suggest that they could continue to dwell in this space in which she was captive? Might it suggest that it might not be essential after all to ascend from their current unsatisfactory altitude and move to another higher plane?

Since Goran and Ana had travelled to Moscow where Ana's discomfort had become trauma, since he had asked her which part of madman Jacob's charge had been untrue, he had decided to embark upon a campaign in which he would move gradually from a position of refusing to defend her father to one in which he would make clear that Bosnian Serb Army activities in Bosnia were unacceptable, that her father was in large part to blame for misery, suffering and multiple deaths there, and that it was he who was trapping her in anguish and torment, unable to reconcile her altruism and humanitarian ambitions with her bloodline. But Goran would bring her round delicately, like the helmsman of a small boat nosing into harbour, then gently nudging to a stop against the boardwalk. He would bring her to a position in which she would acknowledge that she was not a prisoner of her family tree. She needed to step resolutely from beneath it. He, Goran, would provide the boughs that would shelter her and enable her to grow. He was all she needed, but he could only nurture her and they could only grow together if she broke the bloodline. She needed to make a declaration; to tell her father that she was no longer his daughter; to tell him that she renounced him.

And earlier that day, seven weeks on from the shelling of Markale marketplace that had affected Goran so deeply, they had reached the point at which she had had to make that choice. He had hesitated on the brink because he could hardly bear to countenance the possibility of her making the 'wrong' choice, but he had to force the issue, he knew. He had to force it by issuing the ultimatum: him or me.

As the words had fallen from his lips, Ana, perhaps one metre in front of him, had looked up at him in what appeared to be disbelief. She had whispered, "You can't mean this, Goran…" She had looked down at the floor and then back up again. "Can you?"

At that moment, he had noticed the almond shape of her eyes. He was appalled by this collision between her beauty and what an outsider, unaware of the psychological journey they had travelled together, might see as his cruelty. But he clung to his tactics. It wasn't just that he wanted no association with Ratko personally, wanted no one to be able to accuse him of condoning his potential father-in-law's actions; it was Ana's only means of escape. He hoped he had led her subtly, gradually, gently to such a conclusion.

Ana's phone rang. And it rang and rang. She must be home by now. She was choosing not to answer it. Should he go round regardless? No. He would leave her to sleep away as much of her distress as she could overnight and go to see her first thing tomorrow.

12

Goran knocked at the door. No response. No sound of movement inside. He knocked again. After a further minute, he turned the door handle. Unusually, the door opened. Ana usually kept the door on the chain when he wasn't there.

And there she was. Sitting on the right of the sofa as he faced it, directly opposite the front door, slumped to her right, her head tipped, left ear on top, right ear underneath, her chin above her right leg. Blood trails from her nose and mouth had thickened on her upper lip and chin. They had spilled and coagulated on her jeans and the carpet. There was a pistol that he recognised on the floor to Ana's left.

"No-o-o-o, Ana... No-o-o-o... Not this..." It was between a whisper and a cry.

He took a few paces forward till he stood to the right of the sofa and he could see the bullet hole, clean and neat, above her left ear. For a few moments, he looked at the wound clinically. And he recalled his tutor at medical school saying to him, as he prepared to use a surgeon's knife for the first time, "Goran, to repair flesh, you have first to cut into it. Always remember that." And Goran knew that the bullet would have penetrated but nestled in Ana's brain. How long had she been there? Goran thought perhaps one hour, more likely two.

He hunkered down by the arm of the sofa. Ana's slack jaw stripped her of some of her beauty, he thought. And then a wave of panic broke within him and the scale of the implications of the scene before him washed in. The clinical was banished.

He had given her a choice. Two options. And she had conjured up a third – one he could never have framed or envisaged. And one of his voices said, as if out loud, *You did it. You made her do it.* Another voice said, *No, no. You were trying to liberate her. You were trying to free her. You were trying to give her a life.* And he looked at her father's pistol, now on the carpet just in front of him. This was grotesque imagination: Ana not only framing a third option but choosing that weapon to do the deed. It had been in a case in the family home and her father had said he would only fire it in celebration, when a grandchild was born. Oh, this country and its guns! Guns and death everywhere.

Goran breathed in deeply. He had all the time he wanted with Ana now, and he had no time. This was where they had learned to love one another, and now, in an hour or so, it would look like a crime scene. Forensic experts in alien outfits would be marking out key outlines: where Ana was or had slumped, where the pistol fell, where the blood spots had sprinkled. Goran wanted to hold that time between them for a little longer. He couldn't touch her, but he couldn't yet pick up the phone and call the emergency services.

He felt a great hollow open, as the reality that their relationship had gone began to sink in. *No, it can't be*, said one of his voices. And he remembered his favourite moment after their lovemaking, when he would sit back on his heels and look down on her. And he would always lay both hands just inside her hips, where her abdomen joined the tops of her legs, either side of the pubic hair she kept trimmed in a neat triangle. And he would smile down on her. And she would smile back that giving smile; the smile that radiated from the photo of her on the table in her parents' living room. In it she was standing behind her seated father, her arm draped around him, her mother to her right. The very picture of a happy family. And in those post-coital moments when Goran had gazed down on her, Ana would shut her eyes, overcome by a sudden pang of shyness. But the smile would linger. And he would press his hands on her again. Then he would unfurl and lay his head on her hillock breasts. And their souls would well with silent love for one another. *Never again*, his inner voice said. Then, more slowly, *Nev-er again*. He had to try to banish the thought before it overwhelmed him. He leaned over and stroked her bobbed hair, knowing that that was the limit of their ultimate intimacy.

And then the fear began to flood in. Her father would have him killed if he learned of the ultimatum he had given Ana: "Me or him? Renounce your father or I walk away." Was there a suicide note? Had she put something in the mail to her father to explain?

His brain was jamming with the rush of signals emotional and practical. He could spin it out and stay with her awhile. He could flee; pretend he'd never been here. No, no. He couldn't do that. He stood up and then slowly paced around the sofa. If he could just go back and not so much put it right as never issue his ultimatum…

Why did you have to do that? one of his voices asked critically.

It's easy. We were to move on unblemished from these guns and killings and cruelty. To live a pure life, a healing life…

Neither of his voices would prevail. The altruistic voice would never quite eclipse the voice of guilt. And, even at that moment, with blood just clotted on the floor, he knew those two voices would be fighting within him for the rest of his life. No peace. Only regret. And no 'right' road that he could have pursued.

Goran walked around Ana's sofa again, drinking her in as she looked now, twisted and awkward, and drinking in too the images of her that leapt most readily into his mind: of beautiful Ana, of kind Ana, of Ana who wanted to heal others.

He walked to the telephone, heard the whirr of the line, and dialled 194. "Ambulance, please, urgently. It's a fatality." Then Goran dialled another number. "Dragan? Is that you? Listen, it's urgent. I haven't called the police yet but I need you to let the chief of police know before anyone else: it's Ratko's girl… Yes, my Ana… She's dead."

13

Goran had stayed overnight at his parents' home, and his mother's demonstrations of concern for him had been unfussy and without intrusive questioning. After the relatively spartan conditions of his student flat not much more than a mile away, he had enjoyed the comfort, the space and the familiarity of his childhood home as best he could, given the circumstances. However, the temptation had been non-existent to reveal to his parents that it was his ultimatum that had most likely prompted the funeral that would take place on a hill forty minutes' walk away later that morning.

He still couldn't delineate where shock and grief met. Not that it mattered, because their combined weight bore down on him every waking moment. They surrounded every thought with a frame of grey – like the mind of a depressive, who wakes up to find to his or her despair that today is one of those grey days. He might feel a momentary flash of relief as something inside him suggested it couldn't be true, she couldn't be gone forever, it was all a bad dream. But he had had enough waking hours to know that this was delusion, and each flicker of bogus hope was quickly extinguished.

The only other sensation to find any headspace was fear. He kept expecting a call or a knock on the door, followed by the revelation of the discovery of a suicide note. If such a note existed and the details of his ultimatum to Ana were contained within it, he knew that Ratko would kill him or – more likely – have him killed. Despite the events of the last few weeks, Goran didn't want to die – and, unsurprisingly, the prospect of a brutal, drawn-out, score-settling execution terrified him. But so far, no call, no knock at the door. He was still actively considering the possibility of fleeing Belgrade after the funeral – but where would he go, and why abandon his studies if there were no evidence of any threat to his safety? Retribution might come swiftly and without warning, he acknowledged, but second-guessing it might be to overstate its likelihood.

The collar and tie to which he was so unaccustomed chafed at his neck, and he ran a finger round the inside of his collar. Would the coat over his jacket make him too hot, or would he be too chilly without it? Every minute detail appeared an irritant, dragging him down a little further. The natural optimism that he cherished as an attribute was under heavy siege.

As he walked up the hill south from Senjak, he reflected that, although he would not have wanted to be part of the Mladić funeral cortège, no invitation had been extended by the family for him to join them in one of the official cars. How might they view him in future weeks and months? An extended member of their family who might have loved Ana almost as much as they, her flesh and blood? Or an irrelevance now that she was gone, who would soon be nothing but a dim recollection?

As he began to leave behind the residential area and to walk along the edges of the thin woods on the way up to Topčider, Goran was clear that he had no desire to prolong any relationship with any of the three remaining Mladićs. He felt a little for Bosa, he admitted. He had seen at first hand how she had to manage Ratko's volatility. He had no interest in Darko, who he saw as sharing some of his father's boorishness without any offsetting intellect of note. And of course, both Goran's ultimatum to Ana and his strong desire ever since he had been introduced to Ratko to have nothing to do with him were incontrovertible evidence of his desire to sever all relations with the head of the family. And not only would Ratko not crave an ongoing relationship with him, Goran; he wouldn't even think about it. A dandelion pappus to be blown away on the wind. And the thought came to him, not for the first time since Ana had died: how would Ratko have reacted to Ana – and to him – had she chosen his, Goran's, preferred route and renounced her father? Perhaps he, Goran, would have been in a position as parlous as he would be should a suicide note turn up.

But it was too difficult a thought to deal with in any detail at the moment. He tried to suppress it by taking in the trees and the birds flitting among them. Woodpeckers tapped as rhythmically as master carpenters. A pleasing distraction. Weak sunshine was prevailing over partial cloud cover and he was now carrying his coat over his arm. After his woodside walk, the road jagged over a small bridge and a river shrunken to a stream, past rocks daubed with graffiti tags devoid of political messaging, and then up an incline until the lower end of the cemetery came into view.

Goran had visited Topčider Cemetery several times before for a range of interments and he had always admired its grandeur of location. Topčider's splendour was that it was set on a hilltop on a piece of land that tilted downwards, improbably sharply, from south to north. At times it seemed as sheer as forty-five degrees, but realistically it was more like thirty. Nevertheless, it meant that, from the southernmost edge of the cemetery, there were views right down to the bridges over the Sava and into the New Town district of the city.

For Goran, Topčider's unlikely charm was enhanced by headstones crammed close, stretching out like domino lines, teeming with stories part told, pricking the curiosity of the unrelated passer-by. As was the Serbian way, they bore elaborate headshots and tight pen portraits: economists; entrepreneurs; politicians; gangsters, undercover beneath their slabs, their deeds alluded to but understood only by those in the know; young tykes who had lived hard and died young; infants snatched from their parents too young, with insufficient headstone space to do anything but hint at their tragic little lives and deaths.

As Goran entered the top gate, the thought struck him that he was glad that, if Ana had to go – *did* she have to go? – that she should end here. He didn't know yet where her plot would be in this crowded graveyard, but he took some consolation from the thought that, if the dead could see, she would be looking down on the southern quarters of Belgrade, her ghostly twenty-twenty vision capable perhaps of drilling through to Senjak and even to Čolak Antina. He chided himself gently for that sentimentality: *Shit – you don't even believe in the afterlife!* But he acknowledged the warm glow that the thought had flushed through him.

His reverie was brought to an abrupt halt as he entered the main gate and saw the crowd of mourners in dark coats and military garb congesting the path beside the chapel and the administrative buildings of the cemetery. Again, just as at the impromptu barbecue at the Mladić family home a couple of years earlier, he hoped to be able to linger on the fringes rather than be drawn into the centre of the 'event'. There would be no Milan to act as his foil this time – this was not an occasion for him – but he hoped to insinuate himself into a location near enough to witness the details of the proceedings without being part of them.

He nodded to people he didn't know, and the size of the congregation suggested to him that many were there because they felt they needed to be seen to be present because of Ratko's status. He picked out very few of Ana's college friends among the crowds, and he wondered whether the horror of her deed and the notoriety that had contributed to it might have scared away some of those who would have liked to have attended. The presence of journalists in the faculty straight after Ana's death, trying to discover the story behind the story, was likely to have spooked more of them. It had certainly unsettled him.

There was always something excruciating about the wait for the start of an interment. A fear of irreverence cast a silent pall over the gathering. Only essential requests – for a handkerchief or a time check – seemed appropriate, and, as time passed, the gloom deepened. Goran almost felt like screaming to puncture the suffocating near-silence.

As he tried to edge his way into a good vantage point, a man he had nudged turned to him. He smiled benignly as Goran raised a hand in apology. He had a couple of teeth missing and his hair, tied back in a ponytail, gave him a gypsy appearance. His grey pinstriped suit looked like a relic dug out from a wardrobe after years without an outing. His shoes, scuffed at the toes, hadn't seen polish for years. And Goran realised, with a mild sense of horror, that this man was dressed out of character. He was a Chetnik, one of a group of right-wing Serbian nationalists whose popularity had enjoyed a resurgence in the post-Tito years. They believed that around two thirds of Yugoslavia should be incorporated into a Greater Serbia, and, as a result, as he had gobbled up more and more Bosnian territory Ratko Mladić had become something of a hero to them. How repulsive that Ana's funeral should attract racist nationalists because they admired her father, Goran thought.

The man in the faded suit looked uncomfortable because the 'uniform' of choice of the Chetnik in recent years had become jeans, long hair – often tied with a bandana – and a black skull-and-crossbones T-shirt bearing the words 'For King and Fatherland – Freedom or Death'. The Chetniks lacked the organisation of paramilitaries, but they hung out in the streets of Belgrade, selling regalia, and ventured to conflict hotspots on the lookout for a rumble at which they could mete out instant 'justice' to anyone they saw as a political or ethnic foe – perhaps a Croat or a Bosnian Muslim.

"Friend of the family?" the Chetnik whispered to Goran.

"College friend of Ana," Goran replied, downplaying his status.

"Commiserations, pal." The Chetnik swapped his cigarette from his right to his left hand and plunged a dive-bombing handshake down into Goran's hand and shook it firmly.

"Thanks, mate," said Goran.

The pall-bearers emerged from the chapel with Ana's coffin, expertly balancing on its surface abundant bouquets of white flowers. Goran had manoeuvred himself alongside the Chetnik into a space opposite one of four open-fronted, covered bays with trestles where Ana's coffin was to be displayed so that the congregation could circulate to pay their last respects before she was laid in the ground.

The select few that had been in the chapel for a brief service followed the coffin; Ratko at the front, his right hand laid stiffly over his left in front of him, as though he didn't quite know how to present himself in the moment. Goran had expected black jacket, white shirt and black tie for Ana's father but, bizarrely, he had chosen to offset his black jacket with a brown open-necked shirt. Ratko took up a position to the right of the coffin with Bosa to his right. Darko propped a framed photograph of Ana on the lid of the coffin before taking his place at its head. Goran recognised the picture, a handsome portrait which captured her looking to her right: clean features, piercing brown eyes, hair parted in the centre, cut in a neat bob and tucked behind her ears. Every time he had looked at the picture, which had been in the living room of Ana's parents' home, he had noticed the single lock of hair that escaped from the body of the cut and fell across her forehead above her left eye, and every time the

French word for a lock of hair – 'une mèche' – had popped into his mind. Although he preferred her elf-like cut with the side parting, he loved that photograph, and he yearned to steal it after the ceremony and to give it pride of place in his flat. He knew, however, that that would be impossible.

Bosa locked her hand round Ratko's right elbow, as if it was his grief that needed to be managed rather than a shared grief. Goran read Ratko's expression as either blank or stunned, but it wasn't easy to divine which. Three army colleagues in camouflage fatigues made their way round the coffin, each wielding further extravagant bouquets of white flowers; each stopping to give first Ratko, then Bosa, and then Darko the three-kiss salutation: left cheek, right cheek, then left again. As they exited the scene, Ratko laid his head, forehead flat, on the lid of the coffin. At last, he seemed to be letting go his emotions. Bosa clasped his hand behind his back. He remained with his forehead pressed against the coffin lid for some time in silence. Even from his viewpoint ten yards away, Goran felt the tension in the situation. It was as if Ratko had instinctively drawn all the emotional focus upon himself, marginalising others' sorrow and hurt. And Goran realised in that moment an imperative that Mladić had created by his demeanour and his personality over the years: wherever he was in his world, he became the focus. Everyone else was reduced in his presence. Goran felt that he achieved that by spinning around himself an unspoken, perpetual aura of menace. Even though, logically, in the Mladić home he should have been safe, Goran had nevertheless feared almost at every moment Ratko tipping into a sudden act of violence, as if his fists were permanently twitching and ready to slug.

In the tense moments while Ratko kept his forehead pinned to the coffin lid, Goran felt that Ana's father was sucking all the available emotion from this tragic scene in his own direction. He had spent years acting as the towering, dominant figure in the family, so none of his family would have felt in any way eclipsed or deprived of their slice of the grief. This was just how things were in the Mladić family.

Ratko was silent for what seemed like a long time but was probably just twenty to thirty seconds. And then a sound emerged, and then another: first a single sob; then what sounded like a low moan. Bosa stepped in, as if Mladić's moan signalled that it was time to lever him up from his prone state across the coffin. His face returned to view, but there was no crumpling of his features in grief as he rose. His mouth was fixed straight, his eyes he dabbed at with a paper handkerchief, but they showed no loss of control. Bosa clung to his left arm; another woman – was it his sister? – clung to his right. He then began wiping with his handkerchief the coffin lid on which he had shed tears. It was like the gesture of a house-proud housewife, carrying out a task meticulously, almost obsessively.

After ten minutes or so, the family group edged away from the coffin to allow the rest of the congregation to circulate round it. Goran patiently waited his turn and, as he took a closer look at the framed photograph on the lid, he kissed his right fingers and laid them on the coffin. If the gesture was inadequate, he didn't feel that this was his final farewell. As he stepped away from the coffin he felt hollowed out, incapable of tears. And he wondered how long it might be before he felt tranquil again.

Ratko was absorbed in his own grief and looking away, but Darko stepped out of the family huddle and offered his hand. "Thanks for coming, Goran," he said.

Goran looked him in the eye. He hoped that Darko could not read in his expression the antipathy that he felt towards him. "That's okay. It's the least I could do," he replied. If Darko had been able to see the thought bubble coming from Goran's head, he would have read, *Did you think for an instant that I might not come? Idiot!*

There was more excruciating silence and waiting; then at last Darko scooped the photograph from the coffin lid, and the pall-bearers returned, hoisted the coffin onto their shoulders, and strode rhythmically to Ana's final resting place. The crowd around the graveside was ten deep and there was no way that Goran could witness the heartbreaking moments as the pall-bearers let the ropes slip through their hands and the coffin dipped out of sight. There were final prayers and some muted sobbing. Goran stood by a bench on the fringes of the crowd. He would be patient and wait till most of the congregation had dispersed before he had his final moments with Ana.

By the time he was able to approach the grave, the coffin lid was all but covered with clods of earth tossed in by friends and family. He crumbled a fistful of orange clay soil in his hand and sprinkled it gently. "Bye-bye, my lovely Ana," he whispered. And then his tears fell. Not the breaking of a dam of tears – more a gentle flow. "You didn't have to go, you know," he said quietly.

It was hard to drag himself away but, thirty minutes later, he felt he had to go. "I'll be back… soon… often, Ana," he said, and he headed for the cemetery gates before beginning his trudge back down the hill. He felt devastatingly alone.

It took another full month before Goran convinced himself that there was no suicide note. The forensics team would have been scrupulous in their search for anything in Ana's flat that might have provided some kind of motive for her action. Nothing had turned up, and the flat had now been cleared. It meant that the only way in which his secret would emerge now would be if he told someone.

The time that had passed before he was clear about that had enabled him to think through what it all meant. He had landed some conclusions but, alongside, there remained some profound questions that he felt might echo around the halls of his life for the rest of his days. His principal conclusion was troubling in its starkness: all those who had believed that they knew Ana, and loved her because of what they knew of her, clearly had not understood her at all. Even after Moscow, she had clung to Goran in their bed and he could not conceive anything other than that they were tight in a mutually loving space. She would clamber over her father when she went home, and his glow demonstrated how important she was to him. Her mother's thrill at the prospect of their family producing its first doctor saw Mrs Mladić almost fit to burst with pride. And yet none of them had read her. None of them had had the slightest instinct that she was on the brink. Sad, yes. Troubled, yes. Goran could sense both, but he had been a million miles from imagining that, if he offered her him or her father, she would choose a bullet to the temple instead.

How alone must she have felt to be so little understood? And there were further questions. What was the significance of her father's ceremonial pistol? Was it a pointed commentary on this country and its guns? Was it a detail designed to make the hurt her father felt still more keen? Or was it quite simply the only weapon she could lay her hands on that would insert a fatal bullet into her brain?

Another question: was her action punishment or escape? And if it were punishment, who was she trying to punish? Goran or her father? Or was the truth still more poignant? She loved Goran and her father so much she simply couldn't choose between them. Goran had hoped – had he perhaps expected? – that her father's heinous actions – undeniable; regularly blazed over the Press and media – would be enough to tilt the balance his way. He had been wrong.

And another question: was her taking her life bravery or cowardice? Did she side with Goran but lack the courage to face up to her father? Goran could have understood that, but taking and raising the pistol to her temple, then pulling the trigger, was not the act of a coward. That was bravery beyond anything Goran could summon.

And still more questions: had he, Goran, offered up too bluff an aspect to encourage her to share her feelings? Should he have mined her psyche more intrusively? Should he have defied her taboo and talked about the war with a view to making her talk about the war?

A further question hung dauntingly above him. He could barely bring himself to address it. Would she inevitably drift away from him? It was now clear that she had left no trace of anything she had felt about her intolerable position. She had left no written document outlining her feelings or describing her inner turmoil. She had shut him out of her internal debate. She had shared her feelings with none of her friends. Goran knew that. He had asked them all; begged them to tell him if they knew anything. Guilt by association, ignominy, shame? The words had never crossed her lips. Only that scream across the lecture hall in Moscow had given any voice to her distress. It meant that all that was left were recollections as substantial as the water in a stream that runs through the fingers but can never be grasped.

At moments he felt as though the questions might drive him insane. They were relentless. They ground him down. They were disturbing his sleep and disrupting his studies. He just wanted relief from them, but as he framed that thought, he felt a pang of guilt. If he killed the questions, might it not hasten her drifting away from him; the edges of the image of her in his mind fraying, its sharpness blurring? He wanted the questions to stop for the sake of his sanity. He wanted them never to stop out of respect for her memory.

Goran was surprised at the uplift he felt a few days later when he answered the phone and it was Milan on the line. The young officer had slotted into and now occupied a space in his life which Goran found genuinely comforting. He didn't want to sound utilitarian about it because he was genuinely fond of Milan even at this early stage in their friendship, but Goran knew that Milan could act as a sounding board as he struggled to come to terms with his situation, in part because their relationship had a freshness about it. They hadn't settled into that phase in which two people lapse into lazy assumptions about each other's views and attitudes. Reflective and empathetic beyond his modest years, Milan was located at a vantage point from which he might provide Goran with an insight he might never have framed himself – even if fully packaged, complete solutions were not available from anyone anywhere.

"I just thought I'd give you a call, Goran, now that the funeral's over. I thought you might have crashed to earth a bit afterwards."

Crashed to earth. It was an interesting phrase, Goran thought. "You know what, Milan? It's as if I've got all the bruises without ever having taken the fall and hit the ground." And he laughed, but without mirth. "I've got to pick myself up and get on with my life... but that moment feels quite a way off still," Goran said.

"It'll take time, Goran. Don't beat yourself up about it. There are plenty of others out there who'll try to beat up on you. Be kind to yourself. If you have to take time out, do it. Your profs, your pals, they'll understand."

Goran hadn't thought about making a conscious decision about taking time out. He had thought that circumstances might have meant his having to flee Belgrade, but now that he had convinced himself that he didn't need to do that, the suggestion that he take time out was at the same time shocking and attractive. His instinctive reaction was to say to himself, *No, you can't do that,* or, *No, you don't need to do that.* But what if those reactions were wrong? On the few recent occasions when he had tried to sit and take in a chapter from *Robbins Basic Pathology,* words like 'pericardial effusion' and 'hemopericardium' had swum before his eyes; his eyes had glazed over at the colour plates in the textbook that just weeks ago he had found fascinating. So perhaps Milan was right? Or might he take time out and then spend all his time mulling over those questions endlessly?

Then the thought became too much for him and he didn't so much discard it as turn over a page. He switched to narrator mode and talked Milan through the events as best he could capture them: discovering Ana; his panic and then calm as he dealt with the death scene in front of him; his conversations with the police. "I was going to say, 'one of the worst moments', but there have been so many worst moments, so let's say that one really bad experience was when journalists arrived at the medical faculty the day after Ana died," Goran said. "Of course, I wasn't there but some of my friends on our course alerted me to the fact that they were sniffing around and asking questions. Did she have a boyfriend? If so, what was he called and where could they find him?

"Everyone was brilliant. From what I can see, not a single one of my fellow students let on about me. About our relationship. Not one. Of course, eventually they came knocking. They must have gone through the list of enrolled students and found me. Said they'd heard I knew Ana. Was I her boyfriend? And you know, Milan, I was worse than Peter, the Apostle. He only denied Christ thrice after the Last Supper. I must have told six journalists that I wasn't Ana's boyfriend. She had been on my course, yes, but I hadn't really known her." As he said the words, he knew that he had had a compelling excuse: had he said what he had really wanted to say to those journalists, he too would be dead. Nevertheless, Goran shook his head – then realised that Milan, down the line, wouldn't be witnessing his gesture of regret. "How bad is that? My soulmate. My would-be life partner," he said.

"It's not bad at all, Goran. They'd have made your life hell – if it could get any worse," said Milan. "You were right to keep your privacy. It's none of their business."

"So you haven't shopped me to your mate Mick on *The Times*, then?" Goran laughed.

"No – not yet!"

Goran felt there was nothing to be lost by asking how Ratko had reacted since he had returned to duty after the funeral. Surely even he would be mollified or chastened to some degree by the loss of his daughter?

Milan said that he had returned to his duties perhaps shockingly quickly. "Obviously, everyone's offered him their condolences, but he doesn't give much away. The peace plan guy, David Owen, he raised Ana's death with him and spoke of his own son's fight against leukaemia. And I thought for a moment that Ratko was going to open up – two fathers talking about stricken children – but then, in a split second, his guard was up again and the moment was gone."

Milan said that a colleague who had known Ratko for years had told him that the loss of Ana would hit him hard because his concern was always for the bloodline. "For him, apparently, it's the women in his bloodline that really matter: his mother, his sister, and Ana. This guy told me that even his wife, and certainly any other woman who married into the family – well, he never spoke about them with the same kind of reverence reserved for female flesh and blood. He said he thought there would be a chasm in his life. 'But he won't let on. I know him. He'll never let on.'"

"So he's said nothing since Ana's death that gives any hint of what he thinks happened and why?" asked Goran. "I heard that he claimed it was one of his enemies that had bumped her off. Made it look like suicide. Which was nonsense, of course. As the one who found her, I know that."

"Yes – I think he did say that in the immediate aftermath, but the guys tell me that the pathologist, a Dr Stanković, offered to carry out a full investigation into the circumstances of Ana's death to determine the truth. Ratko clearly knew it wasn't necessary. He didn't take up the offer.

"One word doing the rounds is that Ratko did arrange for the bullet that killed her to be extracted from her brain. The cops think he wanted it as some kind of macabre keepsake. It sounds implausible but I heard it from a good source."

Goran thought clinically of the incisions required and the delicate tweezers needed to lift the tiny bullet from the cerebral mush. He winced. "So he's not said anything else – about her state of mind; her reasons for her action?"

"Not a thing. Not a thing. And you know what? None of us – and

I mean literally none of us: his aides, his peers, none of us – would ever dare ask him why he thought what happened happened."

"And do you get any sense that he might blame himself for what she chose to do?"

"In those quiet moments, you never know what he might be thinking. He doesn't give anything away. But what I do know is that he would – he *will* – never show any sign of weakness."

Goran thought back to Ratko over the coffin: one concealed sob; one muffled moan. And then a face to the world which spoke of pain, yes, but a pain that he controlled and a grief that took the expression on his face as far as 'taciturn' – but no further. And Goran felt a momentary pang of anger at Ratko's refusal to show to anyone what the nature of his Ana-shaped loss had been. Knowing that his father had died at the hands of Croatian fascists when he was two had coloured Ratko's view of the world, it was plain. But whether the loss of his apparently beloved daughter would nag away at him, whether he would blame himself, or seek to shrug it aside and blame other factors or other people, Goran would never know. And he suspected no one would know. Not even Bosa, nor Darko. That itself was an eloquent commentary about the man. Goran thought it disrespectful to Ana that Ratko showed no grief – just those few moments by the coffin – but Goran let his anger subside. It was futile to hope for change.

Goran was aware of a debate among Mladić-watchers in the Press about whether the loss of his daughter might introduce an element of compassion to his future behaviour, or whether it might harden his view that life was a conspiracy against him and strengthen a belief that he needed therefore to be more ruthless.

Whichever outcome turned out to be accurate, less than two weeks after Ana was cold in the ground, Mladić led an assault on the town of Goražde – a town that should have been inviolate because it was designated as lying within a UN-protected zone. An argument could be made for either viewpoint: Mladić was acting out of a fury fuelled by his recent personal loss; or he was simply returning to the day job with no adjustment to his modus operandi.

Goran felt he could see in this latest phase of conflict evidence of the threats of which Milan had warned. After the Markale marketplace massacre, international pressure had led to the withdrawal of heavy weaponry to sites twenty kilometres outside Sarajevo, and there was a feeling that a more muscular involvement of the US and Russia could be about to bring an end to the war. He recalled Milan's warning that Ratko was terrified of a ceasefire freezing the front lines before he and his forces had succeeded in removing from Bosnian Muslim hands Bosnian towns along the Serb border – notably, Goražde, Žepa and Srebrenica. Still worse, Western leaders might try to bargain down his seventy per cent control of Bosnian territory to less than fifty per cent.

Goran watched the TV coverage as first the outlying villages around Goražde were cleared out by a Bosnian Serb artillery barrage, and then a three-pronged attack was launched on the city centre; tank, artillery, and mortar fire pushing the enclave with its sixty thousand Muslim inhabitants to the brink of falling. Although the enclave never fell completely, Goražde's Muslim population was effectively marooned, with no power and no water-pumping station, as Mladić's men controlled all the high ground overlooking the town. And Ratko's love of brinkmanship was unmistakable: the effrontery of his assault on a protected area led to the UN agreeing to limited NATO air strikes on Mladić's forces; air strikes the UN had always resisted for fear of putting their peacekeeping forces on the ground in peril. So Ratko's forces across Bosnia temporarily detained 150 UN officers to make it clear that NATO bombing of him and his men would expose that vulnerability on the ground. He would order their release after a brief detention, but not before his men had pushed on towards the heart of Goražde.

Despite the casualties suffered, Goran suspected that Ratko might even perversely welcome the bombardment. The image of Ratko as David in the face of the Goliath forces of the West was one that would have appealed strongly to him, Goran knew. And in film clips that screamed of studied indifference towards their critics, Mladić was filmed in an open space on the outskirts of Goražde playing chess with Karadžić, no doubt as bombs were falling on the town.

I bet Ratko won, thought Goran.

14

As the months after the funeral ticked themselves off, Goran felt something unexpected unfolding: his relationship with Ana continued to evolve. At first he couldn't articulate what was happening, but after a while he was aware that he was somehow sustaining a dialogue with her.

Logic, his medical knowledge, and plausibility all told him that death was a hard stop. Nothing existed beyond the grave apart from gradual physical decay, thankfully unseen. There couldn't be some benign – or malign – Creator out there, perpetually calculating league tables of which individuals were set for Paradise and which were missing the cut. And that 'worship' stuff? Only a human kind of logic could suggest that a celestial Maker might require his creations to bring to his feet their prayers, their hopes, their gratitude on a regular, perhaps daily, basis. What kind of Divinity would demand that – particularly as his creations were slipped into this world without so much as a user's manual? Yet here he was, unable to rid himself of the sense that Ana was looking down on him. But that expression – 'looking down'! We needed to rid ourselves of this crazy concept that a Heaven existed somewhere above our heads. Astronomers, telescopes, satellites couldn't locate it. Even if it did exist, why might it be above us?

But wherever she was or wasn't, Ana was undoubtedly influencing Goran's behaviour and his thinking. Not as a moral guardian or as someone who might register disapproval should he misstep; rather, it was as though their discussions about the way forward continued, as if she were not so much steering his actions and his decisions as helping shape them. And it was a dialogue, not edicts issued from some space that offered her superior, supernatural insights. He felt as if his post-Ana activity was not a series of solitary steps but a shared venture.

He suspected that it might be some time before he could share this sensation with someone else. He wasn't sure he had the words to spell out the experience without appearing unhinged, but it was not only vividly real to him: he derived considerable comfort from whatever kind of dialogue it was.

He didn't delude himself into thinking that Ana might become more substantial over time, but it was as if a chemistry they had shared continued to work, like a lab experiment, the elements of which kept on reacting. Might it be the same chemistry between them that he had divined the first time they had met, but which took her a little longer to appreciate? He couldn't say, of course.

There was nothing censorious about it. He didn't feel as if she were looking down – that concept again! – and warning him off certain behaviours or decisions. *Don't continue to think badly of my father. Don't go out with another girl.* No – it was a gentle, supportive dialogue in which he didn't have to speak out loud. His thoughts drifted to her, wherever she was, and he felt hers drift back to him.

In relation to other women, after a respectable period of time he had sensed approaches from two fellow students. The first was from Tara, a slim woman with long, curling blue-black hair and something of a mystic air about her. He had always found her slightly strange and, on the basis of comments from other students and his own intuition, he sensed that she had had some ghoulish reaction to the circumstances of Ana's death and would like to have occupied the space that she had left behind, as much out of a sense of daring and curiosity as out of real feelings for him. It wasn't hard for him to blank that approach without being in any way impolite or insensitive. Another student, Ljubica, might have been more appropriate. Goran had always warmed to her kind face and her red hair that, at its best, appeared to have the texture of finely spun silk, but he just wasn't ready, and with this comforting dialogue with Ana continuing to evolve, he didn't feel like he would be ready for some considerable time – if ever.

But could he see himself remaining single all his life, the spectre of Ana his only intimate companion? He, Goran, who loved humanity and would have yearned to bring into the world new life with his Ana? Even if it would have needed to wait till after the wars were over; till Serbia was back on its feet? Even if any child would have Mladić blood coursing through its veins, with the risks that that might involve? Well, he just couldn't bring himself to answer that question right now – not least because it was a problem to which he did not currently hold all the elements of a solution.

What he did acknowledge in that moment was that he and Ana had enjoyed an intimacy which he was unsure he could ever emulate with anyone else. How would he feel in some moment in the future if he were to share that most intimate act and discover that it lacked the crucial element that had lifted physical love with Ana above the banal?

Goran had read an interview with the son of a novelist whose advice, as his son had been about to embark upon the journey from adolescence into adulthood, had been that it is one thing to have sex, but to have sex with someone you really, really love lifts it to a completely higher plane. And the novelist's son had said that his entire pursuit subsequently became the search for that intimacy coupled with profound love. Goran had read that interview before he and Ana had made love, and the realisation that he didn't need an extended journey to find that kind of coupling was thunderbolt-strong. It was there between him and Ana naturally. It was as if there were two simultaneous sensations inextricably bound: that gentle, physical build-up to climax – a heightening, thrilling ascent to the apex of sensation – at the same time as their spirits seemed to jam together until they locked in ecstasy and mutual adoration. And then that post-coital glow, when it felt as if neurochemicals were producing a fresh cocktail of sensation. Then there was the unbreakable silence between them as both were instinctively aware that an inappropriate word at that moment might tarnish the sacred place they had reached together – magically, thrillingly.

Goran tried to still the persistent questioning in his head. Could he have some respite, just for a short period, he asked? But who was he asking? Godless though he was, was he instinctively turning towards some divine source despite himself? Or were these questions purely internal to himself? He felt as if he was interrogating someone, something – but he let the thought drop. It was too hard to explore.

A couple of months after Ana had been laid to rest, Goran returned for the latest of his regular visits to her grave to find that charcoal-grey slabs had been laid and a headstone raised. He was momentarily shocked by the sense of finality they seemed to impart, but then he appreciated the simple, clean design. One thing stood out: the headstone's understatement. How was that for pure oxymoron, Goran thought? In a cemetery in which the families of many of the deceased appeared keen to catch the eye of the passer-by with the story or image of their loved one, Ana's headstone was virtually alone in omitting any detail of her backstory. Only the name 'Mladić', and then below, in smaller font, 'Ana' and the years of her birth and death, '1971–1994', were etched on it. No reference to her mother or father or brother, no etching on the marble reproducing an attractive headshot of her, no commentary on how 'the deceased' had found herself beneath a marble slab at the age of just twenty-three.

If Goran was initially taken aback by the simplicity of the design and the spareness of the content, as he sat on a bench that had been placed alongside the grave, the more he thought about it, the happier he was that her monument did not moor her to her past. Might it in some way allow her to float free; finally escape that notoriety that her actions suggested she could no longer continue to tolerate?

And then he set to asking how it was that Ratko had been dissuaded from featuring on the headstone, as the father of the deceased. Goran found it hard to countenance, as he recalled the coffin-side scene at which Ratko had tried to monopolise the sympathy directed at Ana's family. Might it be for fear of his foes desecrating the grave? It might be, Goran thought, though he hoped that there were subtler, more noble reasons. At the very least, it might allow him to craft his own version of the significance of the headstone's silence: a slate wiped clean; all associations with a monster removed.

At that moment, perhaps because he had been unprepared for the laying and raising of slab and headstone, he lost communication with her for a period. The dialogue between them came to a halt, but he felt no panic. Once he had adjusted himself to this new situation, she would be back in touch. He knew she would, and he would be back in touch with her.

And so it would prove. Sometimes the line would go dead and the exchange of thoughts would be disrupted, and Goran feared that these might be the first warnings that, at some point, their dialogue would end. But so far, it had held up.

Goran looked down from Ana's grave in section twenty-six of Topčider. She had been laid in a space not far from the chapel and the cemetery's flower shop and administrative buildings, but just about as far south as a plot could be – just thirty metres or so from the perimeter fence. The rest of the graveyard tipped away down the hill, affording an unbroken view through the trees on the edges of the cemetery right down to the New Town. Years later, the stunning cable-stayed Ada Bridge, ninety years in the planning, would be raised in that gap between the trees, linking Čukarica district to New Belgrade across the Sava two kilometres from Topčider. Ana would have been forty when it opened, Goran had reflected. Its single pylon splaying off strings like a harp was a handsome addition to the view from her grave rather than an intrusive development.

Some weeks after the headstone had been raised, Goran's tranquillity on the bench by Ana's grave had been clumsily disrupted. Out of the corner of his eye, he spotted someone walking purposefully past the cemetery buildings, and he realised it was her brother, Darko, about to turn up the hill towards her plot. Goran didn't even take a split second to think. He ducked down instinctively and exited behind the headstone of the adjacent grave, then scurried off along the path that led in the opposite direction to the cemetery gates, like someone fleeing a crime scene. He was sure that Darko would not have been able to see him either by Ana's grave or as he escaped the scene, but when he reached a bench on the far side of the cemetery, way beyond any route Darko might take on his way out, he wondered why it had felt so imperative not to be seen by him and not to engage in any conversation with him. It was better that he drift away from the Mladićs, not least because he really did fear Darko reading the antipathy towards him in his eyes, but more importantly, the arrival of Darko reminded him that Ana had not quite floated free of her notorious associations. The thought challenged his attempt to relocate Ana; to read the understatement of her headstone as a slate wiped clean. The feeling of peace that he had been able to conjure, sitting just feet from Ana, had been broken, and although Goran had no concerns about his ability to recreate the tranquillity he had felt, regrettably, each session would now be hedged with an awareness that Darko or Ratko could appear at any minute. He knew he had to prevent that thought from impinging on his and Ana's shared Topčider space and the comfort he could derive from those private moments by her side. It was too valuable a gift to let go.

There followed several further visits to Ana's grave without the arrival of another Mladić, and Goran had become accustomed to this new arrangement: the bench by the headstone; the view down to the Sava. These days, as best he could, he tried to transmit two messages beyond the grave: she was utterly blameless, and she hadn't had to go. She could have – *should* have – stayed, and walked away from shame. The response he intuited was that it had all been too much. She had been asked to deal with too much.

I'm twenty-three, for Christ's sake, and everyone's expecting me to be sober and mature. It was too much to ask of me, Goran, he imagined hearing her say – but there was a softness and at most a sorrow to her tone; no rancour or anger. Sometimes Ana's voice was thin, nearly scrambled; at other times the radio receiver was sharply tuned and it came on stronger. These words were crystal clear.

I know, I know, Goran replied. And he wondered whether he was tiptoeing towards a regret at his ultimatum that he had not so far conceded.

And then, after months of having no contact with Ratko, thinking of him occasionally but no longer obsessed by him as he had been inevitably in the run-up to and the aftermath of Ana's death, his proxy – Milan – walked through the door. He and Ratko were on a flying visit to Belgrade.

"He's gone to see Slobo," said Milan. "There's all sorts of trouble between Milošević, him and Karadžić. As the Bosnian Army has got stronger and we're taking more of a hit, everybody's squabbling – which makes it even harder to come up with and deliver the right military plan."

Goran made coffee as Milan mooched round his living room, picking up books from the shelves and examining them. Goran sensed that he was nervous to the point of jumpy, and that this was a displacement activity.

"It's mainly boring medical stuff, Milan. You'll not find many of the classics there, I'm afraid," Goran said apologetically.

"I don't know. Nabokov's *Lolita* probably qualifies as a classic these days," Milan mused. "Oh, by the way – is there a pharmacy near here? I've just remembered Ratko needs me to put in a prescription for him. God – he'd kill me if I forgot."

"A prescription?"

"Yeah – dunno what it's for. Heart pills or blood pressure tablets or something. He seemed quite twitchy about them. I think he's running low." And he laughed. "Look at me – I'm like his batman these days."

Milan headed out to the pharmacy just a block away from the flat, then sat down for his coffee on the two-seater sofa opposite Goran.

"So, how are you coping, Milan, if the bosses are fighting each other?"

Milan paused, as if calculating whether to open up or to issue a banality and kill any conversation. "To be honest, Goran, it's not great. I'm not feeling comfortable because I think there's some seriously bad stuff coming down the line. Stuff I don't really want to be part of."

Milan explained that, as the signs of the conflicts being brought to a close by foreign powers grew stronger, the Drina Valley in the east of Bosnia, near the border with Serbia, was looking ever more likely to be a flashpoint. "Ratko's already slackened the Bosnian Muslims' grip on Goražde, even though it was supposed to be a protectorate. But Srebrenica is the real problem."

Ratko's nemesis, Naser Orić, had won a rare Bosnian Muslim victory there early in the war, his men sniping from the hills that ring three sides of the town, killing the Serb mayor and eventually driving out the entire Serb population. "By all accounts it's become a magnet for every Bosnian Muslim fighter in the region. There were six thousand people there before the war. Now that it's a UN protectorate, there are around twenty-five thousand. There's more than forty thousand in the whole Srebrenica enclave. Ratko's desperate to take that whole Drina strip back: Srebrenica, Žepa, Goražde. Now they've even got a name for the operation: Operation Krivaja '95. That's bad because it means there's a plan – not just an ambition. With all those Bosnian Muslims crammed into Srebrenica in particular, I think it's going to be bloody." Milan looked down at the carpet, then back up, fixing Goran with his gaze. "And you know, Goran, I want none of it. None of it. Let's just stop the killing, I say. Draw down the curtain on this whole awful episode." He sighed with exasperation. "But who's going to listen to me? Shit – I'll probably be expected to spin it as a triumph!" He paused again. "I'd love to just walk away from it all… but I can't… obviously."

Goran felt Milan had a lot more to say; a lot more frustration to leak. He wondered to what degree his friend's hero worship of Ratko had been eroded. He no longer sounded like someone still in thrall. But Milan clearly felt he had said enough. He didn't want to open up further.

"Goran, if it's okay with you, I'm going to pop out to a bookshop. I'm out of reading material."

"Sure, sure," said Goran.

"You're all right if I leave my stuff here and pop back before I hook up with Ratko, I suppose?"

"Yeah, yeah – fine."

Goran sat for some minutes eyeing Milan's holdall. He couldn't, could he? He'd be betraying Milan if he took a look, wouldn't he? In the end, the temptation became too strong. *There's nothing wrong with curiosity, is there?* one of his inner voices reasoned.

He unzipped the bag. As well as some toiletries and a few clothes, there was the paper bag containing a box, which contained a vial of tablets that Milan had brought back from the pharmacy. Goran took it out of the box and examined the label to understand the kind of drug contained in the medication. He understood quickly that the tablets were for a heart condition that was frequently diagnosed among men of a certain age and lifestyle. He understood too why Ratko might have been twitchy, as Milan had put it, were he to be running low. Once prescribed, they became critical to a patient's stability of health.

Goran expected that Milan would have headed for one of the bookshops on Kralja Petra in the city centre, so he had plenty of time before his return. He sat for a few further minutes. *You wouldn't, would you?* What had appeared preposterous, impossible a few minutes earlier was becoming more and more of a possibility.

He went into his bathroom and, in the cupboard beneath the sink, located a bottle of plain white tablets and took it out. In the sitting room he checked the number of pills in Ratko's prescription – sixty; enough for two months – and counted out sixty of the tablets from his own container. He held them in his hand. He couldn't, could he?

After perhaps five minutes of deliberation as he weighed up the implications of what he might or might not do, he tipped his white tablets back into their original bottle. He put the vial containing Ratko's prescription back in its box and tried to put it in its paper bag precisely where Milan had placed it in his holdall. He put his own bottle of tablets back in the cupboard beneath the bathroom sink.

When Milan returned, Goran didn't need to try too hard to conceal the fact that he had betrayed his friend's trust by rummaging through his bag. Milan was too excited by the purchases he had been able to make to notice any uneasiness in him.

"I can't believe it! They had the latest Philip Roth!" he said, gazing at the cover of one of his books.

And then he was gone. And Goran sat in his armchair; the question *Should I have?* on repeat in his brain. Eventually, he stood up, went to his desk and opened *Robbins Pathology* in the hope that it might still the question and grant him some peace from his deliberations.

But then another question popped up: *If you had, what would Ana have thought?* And he realised that he had temporarily shut down his dialogue with Ana.

15

It was a couple of months before Goran saw Milan again, and when he did, it was in circumstances that were both shocking and worrying. The shock came from the tap on the door of Goran's flat at just after ten o'clock in the evening. No one called unannounced at that time of night. Then Goran heard Milan's voice, in not much more than a whisper, on the other side of the door.

"Goran, it's Milan. Can you let me in?"

Goran opened the door to find Milan in uniform with a rucksack slung over his shoulder. "Come in, come in," said Goran. "What's happening?" He could read the agitation in Milan's expression.

The worrying aspect came as Milan announced, barely suppressing his panic, "I've quit, Goran. Deserted. I'm on the run."

"You *what?!*" Although, when they had last spoken, Milan had articulated his desire to be out of the army, away from Ratko, and free from any connection to the bloodshed he had forecast, it was still a huge shock to Goran that he had in fact walked – or run – away.

On the international satellite TV stations in recent days, Goran had seen reports of disturbances in the Drina Valley area. His ears had pricked up when he heard Srebrenica mentioned because of Milan's hunch that this town could be the main flashpoint in the area. But reports were vague. The area was simply too dangerous for any journalist other than Serbs accompanying Bosnian Serb army units to venture into, so rumours of serious bloodshed were just that for the moment.

"Goran – sorry to impose on you, and I hope I'm not putting you in any danger, but are you okay if I stay overnight here? I don't know if they'll have noticed yet that I've gone, but if they have, they'll be likely to go first to my folks' place, so I think I'd better stay away from there. No one saw me coming up here; I'm sure of that."

Goran laid a reassuring hand on his shoulder. "Yeah, of course you can. Do you want to lie low here for a while?"

"No – you know, I think I'd better take off first thing tomorrow morning. I've got the makings of a plan, if I can just find a way over the border." Milan explained that his aim was to try to reach Zagreb, which he knew his journalist friend, Mick, was using as his base for his coverage of the wars. "I'm going to see whether Mick might be able to help me reach Britain. Tell the authorities I'm a refugee in fear for my life." He paused. "Which I will be before long…" He struck a rictus grin that contained no mirth.

"Okay," said Goran. "You know you're more than welcome. Now sit down and let me get you a coffee. Or perhaps something stronger?"

Goran unscrewed the cap of his pear brandy and poured a couple of generous slugs. He could sense the impact as Milan took his first sip and the alcohol hit him.

"Boy, that's good," Milan said. He was staring in front of himself, clearly not focusing his gaze on anything, reliving the moments of his decision to flee and then the details of his flight.

"Do you want to tell me what happened?" Goran asked gently. He was concerned for his friend but eager to learn the circumstances that had finally convinced him that flight was right.

His tie ripped off, his jacket on the back of a chair, and his boots parked by the side of the sofa, Milan rested his elbows on his knees and swung the rakija round the glass in his hands. "It had been gradually dawning on me and I suppose I just kept trying to pretend that it wasn't happening. Or that those Muslim villagers were getting what they deserved – for acts of terrorism against us. But it reached a point where I couldn't keep on lying to myself about it," said Milan.

He explained that a pattern had begun to emerge, as the Mladić entourage toured the eastern border where Bosnian Serb forces were tightening their grip. "We would visit a village from where – allegedly – local people were rocketing or shooting at our men, Ratko would talk to the local Bosnian Serb commander, and we'd move on. And then we'd learn later that, fifteen minutes after we'd moved on, the killings had started. It happened at Kravica, Konjević Polje and Nova Kasaba. There comes a point where it can't be coincidence; it has to be a plan."

Milan said that he had already felt the tension rising and Ratko preparing his men for an 'engagement', though he didn't know what form it might take. "We were in the area one evening and he was rallying the troops. And he fired them up. He said, 'At last, after the revolt of the *dahiyas*, the time has come to take revenge on the Turks of this area.' And the men clapped and cheered."

Milan explained that the *dahiyas* had been a group of ill-disciplined janissaries during the Ottoman Empire, who had launched a regime of terror against the Serbs in the second half of the eighteenth century, culminating in the assassination of Serb leaders in 1784. "So this man who I'd enthusiastically followed back in 1991 in Knin because he was convinced that we needed to hold Yugoslavia together, who believed – like Tito – that nationalism was a disaster, was now resurrecting two-hundred-year-old ethnic grudges to justify mass killings."

Milan said that it soon became clear that Ratko was trying to hold two totally contradictory positions simultaneously. So it was clear: one of them had to be a lie. Just a couple of days after Ratko had vowed revenge on 'the Turks', Milan had been with him in the Fontana Hotel in Bratunac, ten kilometres north of Srebrenica. Ratko had arranged to meet a UN Protection Force general in the company of a young Muslim head teacher from a school in Srebrenica. He was called Nesib Mandžić, and Milan suspected he was the only Muslim in the town prepared to meet Ratko. Ratko had explained that he wanted a solution to Srebrenica.

"Ratko was gracious to Mandžić and, in front of the UN general, he promised that, if the Muslim population agreed to lay down arms, they would all survive – even their fighters. I remember his words. He said, 'I guarantee that all those who lay down their weapons will live. I give you my word, as a man and a general, that I will use my influence.'" Milan looked down at the carpet and then back up at Goran. "I think we know now which of his two statements was honest. He gave his word that none would die, but it clearly mattered more to him to 'take revenge on the Turks.'"

"So when did you decide that you had to get away?" asked Goran.

Milan put down his glass, interlocked the fingers of each hand, and looked into the distance, as if imagining himself back at Srebrenica. "The day before our meeting at the Fontana, we took a ride into Srebrenica town. It was virtually a ghost town because half the population had fled and the other half had walked the seven kilometres to Potočari, where there was a UN compound. They were either milling around the UN compound, hoping UNPROFOR would save them, or had been incarcerated in buildings nearby.

"Ratko just wanted to be sure there were no remnants of Muslim fighting forces using the town as a hideaway. We knew Naser Orić had been spirited away a couple of months earlier and was probably lying low in central Bosnia somewhere, so their real danger man wasn't around, but we checked the hospital and other likely hiding places but there were no able-bodied men of fighting age.

"And, as we're walking through the streets, I felt a tug on my sleeve and there was a tiny old woman there in the traditional shawl and headscarf." Milan said that the woman had a weather-beaten complexion, her hands were rough, no doubt from decades of domestic work, and her cheeks sunken into the space where healthy teeth once had been.

"'Please come, sir. Please help,' she was saying, and she drew me over to the door of a small house."

Milan said he had been so surprised by her appearance at his side that he had followed her. He stepped in through the door of her home, and a fat man – her husband, he presumed – was sitting slumped in an armchair, wearing olive-green trousers with braces on top of a white vest. He looked barely conscious, and as Milan took a step or two inside, there was an overpowering stench of human sweat in the unaired room. He could make out fleas picking their way around the man's arms and vest – a huge, barely mobile feast to feed from. The man's breath was wheezy and laboured.

"She said to me, 'Please help. He needs medicine. If he doesn't get medicine, he'll die.' I just remember the guy barely opening his eyes to look at me and then drifting back out of consciousness. And I had to get out of that house because I just couldn't take the fetid atmosphere any more.

"'I'll get help,' I told her."

Milan said he had stepped back out into the street and caught up with the Mladić group again. "I thought I wouldn't bother Ratko with it, so I approached one of his lieutenants. I told him what I'd seen. Said we needed to get help. And he just snapped at me: 'Fuck the *balijas*,' he said. And I was so taken aback. And we cruised around the town on foot for ten more minutes, and then we were into our vehicles and off back to Potočari." Milan breathed out, summoning up the moral strength to complete his tale. "And, as we were driving away, I began thinking about my mother in our comfortable home in Belgrade and it came at me like a rush. I asked myself, *What have I become?* How could I admit to my own mother that I'd abandoned an old lady and her husband like that – helpless and virtually alone in a deserted town? She set us standards as kids that weren't difficult to meet; they were just common decency. And here I was, turning my back on people in need. I knew at that moment that I was becoming – or maybe I'd become – someone I wasn't proud to be. And I either had to face up to the challenge of walking away and all the complications that that might bring with it, or live with the fact that I risked becoming someone I despised."

Goran gave a low whistle in acknowledgement. "So you cut and run? That's brave," he said.

"You know, Goran, I don't think it had anything to do with bravery. I've never been anywhere near this feeling before, but when you think you can't live with yourself any more…" Milan paused, as if he didn't know how to come to terms with the thought, then added, "You have to take drastic action."

Goran's words came out before he realised that he had framed the thought. "Like my Ana…"

Milan left a respectful silence, then said solemnly, "Yes – like your Ana."

Goran let the thought sink in. He had said it almost despite himself. On reflection, he didn't regret framing it or saying it. "So, how bad is it in Srebrenica, Milan? The international media don't seem to have got across it yet."

"Goran, if the pattern follows what I was told happened in smaller villages and settlements, I think it's going to be horrific. Ratko makes these promises, then his men separate the women and children from the men of fighting age. The women and children, they bus away. The men then 'disappear'. If there are no Muslim men left to fight, then you end up with a Bosnian Serb town or village."

"But the 'disappeared' will come back to haunt Ratko and Karadžić, won't they? Like in South America, the 'disappeared' reappear – even if they're corpses in a mass grave," said Goran.

"Well, you'd like to think that, wouldn't you?" said Milan.

"So how many victims are we talking about, Milan?"

"If Srebrenica follows the pattern elsewhere, you're talking hundreds. Maybe even thousands," said Milan.

Goran exhaled in amazement.

"I know. It's shit, isn't it?" said Milan.

Goran left some space in the conversation, as he plucked up the courage to ask the question to which he really wanted an answer. "So, you were pretty struck with Ratko when I first met you. When did you first feel something was wrong?"

Milan sighed and ruffled his fingers through his hair. "You have to remember that, when I first met him, he wanted to hold Yugoslavia together and, like me, he abhorred nationalism. When I landed, he really was loved by the men. I've seen other sides to him since, but there was no doubt he was hugely brave. He knew how to inspire loyalty. But then he justified his change of allegiance by saying that, once Croatia and Slovenia had broken away, there was a risk that it was the Serbs again who would suffer in any new carve-up. He had this line about how, throughout history, the Serbs made the sacrifices and then got the worst deal. And he couldn't let it happen again."

"And did you agree with that?"

Milan paused and looked aside. He looked back at Goran. "No – not really. I knew we couldn't patch the Federal Republic back together again, but I didn't really believe there was any conspiracy against the Serbs. But then Ratko was bringing me closer and closer into the fold. He made me feel good about myself. I think he thought I was smart. And to be honest, most of the time we were winning. We were doing a good job."

"You mean militarily – not morally?" asked Goran.

Milan paused again. "Well, I can say that now but…" His voice trailed away. He looked back at Goran. There was a slight pleading to his tone. "Goran, it was a job. I'd known nothing else: military college and then service. Sometimes I might have felt uncomfortable about things – Sarajevo; how some Muslim villages were emptied – but… how can I put this? I had nowhere to go. I was stuck. Desert and you face a court martial at best… like I do now."

The phrase 'I had nowhere to go' leapt out at Goran, like a sudden cry echoing in a valley. It elicited sympathy and convinced him that Milan needed to be spared further scrutiny. He needed to ease off his inquisition, much though he was fascinated by Ratko and the spell he cast upon those around him.

It was close to midnight and Goran suggested that Milan might want to turn in if he was planning an early start.

"Yes, I'd better, I suppose. I'll need one more favour, though, if it's okay. Could I borrow a set of clothes? I need to shed this uniform if I'm to make it over the border." And he laughed.

Goran dug out of his wardrobe a checked shirt that he was fond of but with which he was happy to send Milan on his way to his new life, whatever that might hold. He found jeans too, and an old bomber jacket; each item of a style that would mean Milan didn't look swamped, given that he was of a slighter build than Goran.

"If I don't see you in the morning, Goran, you need to know I'm eternally grateful to you – whatever happens to me. And I'll be in touch."

Milan held out a hand. Goran stepped in and wrapped his arms around him. The least he deserved was a man-hug.

"Make sure you do, Milan. And godspeed!" The divine reference was out before he realised it.

The rakija helped Goran tumble into a deep sleep, and he felt a pang of regret when he woke to see that the time was 8.45am and that Milan had gone. His military boots stood abandoned by the sofa; his uniform folded over its arm.

In the years until Goran next saw Milan, he would keep the uniform in a drawer and the boots would stand in the bottom of his wardrobe alongside his own street shoes. He would never have contemplated removing them. And often, as he opened his wardrobe and saw them, he would smile at the sentimentality that led him to afford them their own space in his day-to-day life.

Sometime later, Goran would read that, after virtually the totality of the Bosnian Muslim population of around thirty-eight thousand people in and around Srebrenica had been removed from the area in the course of five days in mid July 1995, the International Committee of the Red Cross estimated that a total of 7,079 Bosnian Muslims had been killed in fighting, been executed, died fleeing Bosnian Serb attacks, or were otherwise unaccounted for.

Milan's estimate had been way, way too low.

16

Less than a fortnight after Milan's desertion, the International Criminal Tribunal for the former Yugoslavia in The Hague indicted Ratko on the grounds of genocide and other crimes. The indictments related to the siege of Sarajevo, Bosnian Serb-run concentration camps in north Bosnia, and the seizure and use as human shields of UN peacekeepers. Less than four months later, similar charges, including genocide, would be laid against him, specifically in relation to the Srebrenica killings.

Those Srebrenica killings and, a month later, a second bombing of Sarajevo's Markale market, this time leaving forty-three dead and seventy-five injured and this time firmly laid at the door of the Bosnian Serbs, finally prompted Western and Russian leaders to intervene in a meaningful manner and put a stop to the conflicts. The deal was done at a meeting in Dayton, Ohio. The peace that Goran, Milan and millions more had craved was achieved – though, exasperatingly, two, three or four years too late for many of the conflicts' victims.

The scale of the genocide at Srebrenica became public only gradually in the days and weeks after the events. Despite his having witnessed Ratko at closer quarters than many, even Goran struggled to take in the scale of the depravity that Ana's father had fostered there. And if Ana were really somewhere out there and their dialogue was not simply a creation of Goran's subconscious, what might she be thinking from her place of rest? It was fatuous to create league tables of atrocities, but there was no doubt that the scale of the Srebrenica slaughter was right up there with the worst in Europe since the Holocaust. It amounted to barely any kind of counterbalance, but at least it appeared that Ratko could now be hauled before an international tribunal. Early speculation was that it might even bring a life sentence.

The question kept firming in Goran's mind: had she lived, how might Ana have been able to cope with the associated shame from these latest, unspeakable deeds? Uncomfortable though the thought was, might she have been spared unimaginable, additional ignominy by departing the scene one year before Srebrenica, even if there was no way she could have anticipated anything on its scale? Goran had despised Ratko before. Words couldn't describe his reaction to him after these 'exercises' in the Drina Valley. He hated the deepening stain Ratko laid across the memory of Ana. Post-Srebrenica, Goran yearned to be the guardian of her reputation; to distance her from her father in the public eye. But what could he do – a college acquaintance; a partner with no public profile – to ensure she was never associated with her crazed, now clearly genocidal father? He had no idea – but it wasn't a pursuit he was prepared to give up.

Meanwhile, a less urgent, contextual question chipped away at him persistently: how could it be that this sweetest of people, intent on pursuing a caring profession, had been sired by this man? Had her paternal grandfather, the father Ratko had never known, been cut from different cloth? Might he have had Ratko's bravery, but grounded in a more altruistic heart? He had fought with the Partisans against German, Italian and Croatian fascists. How likely was it that his death, when Ratko was just an infant, had skewed his son's psyche? Highly likely. A boy growing up in poverty with no father to give him moral guidance. Had he survived, might Ratko's father have shown him a more caring path; softened those boorish edges? Of course we couldn't say, but he might have. If that might be a generous potential concession, it was one of the only explanations that Goran could frame that might go some way towards explaining the moral gulf between his Ana and her father.

He wasn't surprised that the Srebrenica episode created radio silence between him and Ana for a while. How could he expect her to communicate, profoundly or banally, against such a backdrop? Again, he was sanguine about this. Had they still been together, Srebrenica would have either prompted a crisis between them, or perhaps tipped Ana over into territory to which he had beckoned her: *Renounce that man.* Surely she couldn't have stuck by her father after that?

There was radio silence too from Milan, though Goran was unsurprised by that. Milan had set himself high hurdles to leap and significant ingenuity to conjure up if he were to make it to a safe place. Yet Goran thought about the callow nineteen-year-old he had met on the lawn at Ana's parents' house in Belgrade, and the slightly savvier yet still idealistic young man to whom he had lent his checked shirt and wished godspeed, and he was hopeful that Milan might have been able to summon up sufficient practicality to marry with his undoubted intelligence. Goran craved a positive outcome, and he felt he was transmitting to the ether or to some other unspecified place the lay equivalent of prayers for the safe passage of Milan. Perhaps he was holed up in a hiding place, or even in a hotel room in Zagreb, reading Philip Roth's *Operation Shylock: A Confession* – the novel he had been so thrilled to pick up and tuck into his holdall, alongside Ratko's heart pills, on his penultimate visit to Belgrade.

After the news of the indictments, Goran had expected things to move relatively quickly, but he was to be profoundly disappointed. Serbian military and Bosnian Serb lieutenants' protection regimes, together with international inertia, combined to enable Ratko to avoid arrest, according to reports. The word was that he was continuing to live a life featuring significant stints in the family home in Banovo Brdo, as well as making trips in plain sight to restaurants and football matches in Belgrade.

Goran would hear later from Milan's journalist father that Ratko had been tucked away for periods in gated, guarded holiday homes for Yugoslav military top brass – first in Rujac, 160 kilometres south of Belgrade, and then Stragari, one hundred kilometres south; luxurious billets where he could walk in the woods, swim, play tennis, and enjoy fine catering. When in Belgrade, while it might have looked as though he was swanning around hotspots and sports events carefree, members of a hundred-strong unit from the Bosnian Serb Army were watching him, guarding him, and ensuring he wasn't snatched, given that he had a five-million-dollar bounty on his head.

And there were further distasteful developments that suggested Goran's hopes of swift justice might be moonshine. Graffiti was popping up across the concrete spaces of Belgrade: '*Srpski heroj – Ratko Mladić*' ('Serb hero – Ratko Mladić'). The words were often accompanied by the same spray-paint stencil of Mladić's head and shoulders – instantly recognisable from photos of him in his Bosnian Serb Army cap. Tasteless chants celebrating the massacres at Srebrenica were also heard on the terraces of Red Star Belgrade's football ground – the club that had provided a conveyor-belt supply of nationalist thugs for Arkan, the leader of the notorious Serb paramilitary group, the Tigers.

The dialogue that Goran had resumed with Ana tiptoed around Srebrenica but, with his medical training coming to an end, he was beginning to consider the route he might take after qualifying. And he was attempting to sound out Ana on the right way forward. What might she have advised? Where might they have gone together? In his bed at night, he did not so much whisper to her as float his thoughts out to her domain. Whether it were true dialogue, or more likely, their history packaging automatic messages back to him, what came back felt substantial. It was useful material. He could work with it. And he tried not to slant it to fit his preferences.

Darko had told him, on that fateful night before Goran found Ana dead in her flat, that she had talked about quitting her studies and going as a nurse to the front line in Bosnia to treat wounded Bosnian Serb combatants. This was a second-hand account and, if it were hard to believe that Darko would have made up that detail, Goran believed that, if she *had* uttered it, it was at a time when her mind was imbalanced and she couldn't think straight. Now that the war was over, what if he were to go to Bosnia? Had she lived, might he have been able to persuade Ana to go, so that they could make together some kind of reparation to the Yugoslav state most ravaged by the wars? Early in their relationship, when he had suggested that they might spend their early years after qualifying in field hospitals in Africa, she had suggested that there was sufficient need in remote, poor pockets of Yugoslavia to occupy them. Now, after the devastation of the conflicts, there was even more to do at home. What about focusing on children – children wounded physically or psychologically in the wars? Surely Ana would sign up to that.

Goran had read about Tuzla in central Bosnia. It was the size of a medium-sized town across much of the rest of Europe, but it was Bosnia's third largest 'city'. Renowned for its strong, interethnic institutions and associations, it had been virtually unique across Bosnia as a municipality in standing firm against threats of ethnic division during the conflicts. Despite some attempts by radicals and nationalists to hijack it, strong leadership and the support of business and financial leaders galvanised popular support behind an inclusive, non-partisan Tuzla municipal government. In the middle of the war, Tuzla had come to Europe-wide attention, winning the Alfonso Comin Award, a prestigious international recognition of prominent defenders of justice, peace and human rights. The award brought with it Western humanitarian aid, sparing Tuzla from the need to accept Islamic aid from external sources, which may have had undesirable strings or associations attached.

He had read too of how, after tens of thousands of Muslim refugees from Srebrenica and the rest of the Drina Valley had descended on the city, its leadership had provided safe harbour for them, but then resisted their appeals for the Bosnian Serbs who had remained in the town to be expelled. Every individual who signed up to democratic means was welcome to stay, their mayor, Selim Bešlagić, had insisted. Shortly afterwards an Interreligious Council of Bosnia and Hercegovina, led by Muslim, Orthodox Christian, Catholic and Jewish leaders, was established. Now the Christian charity with a focus on the welfare of children, World Vision, was working on the ground in Tuzla in cooperation with the Interreligious Council. Might Goran find a place alongside them – a Belgrade doctor working to help Bosnian children? He felt he could have led Ana along that pathway.

As he was considering whether he had the courage to choose that step rather than multiple other more comfortable options, a letter landed bearing the unmistakable, neat handwriting of Milan. So he had made it! He was safe. But where was he?

Goran tore open the envelope and, to his delight, he found three sheets of densely covered writing paper. Around eighteen months had passed, so there was likely to be much to tell.

Milan told how he had hitched a series of rides north until he had reached the Fruška Gora national park, south-west of Novi Sad.

I had to come up with a story about who I was, so I said I was a student from the medical faculty in Belgrade called Goran, going back to my family home. I hope you don't mind!

He had crossed the park, then travelled by night by torchlight for forty-eight hours until he had crossed the border into Croatia and finally reached Osijek, where he was able to take a bus to Zagreb.

Thankfully, Mick was in situ in the Hotel Astoria. I'd remembered him saying that he always stayed there when he was in Zagreb. Top man – he put me up in the hotel for a few days, while he made enquiries about whether he could get me to England.

Milan said that he thought Mick had been very clever because he had let the authorities know that they had an opportunity to interrogate someone who had worked closely with Ratko Mladić.

He told me he told them I might be able to give them some evidence and some insider information that could be fed to the prosecution team when Ratko finally does get hauled up before the tribunal in The Hague.

So, when I got off the plane in London, they whisked me off to another hotel, parked a proper British bobby outside my room – I didn't know whether it was for my protection or in case I absconded – and then took me into a building overlooking the River Thames for three days running so that they could debrief me.

Milan said he had been frank to these people he presumed were either MI5 or MI6 officers about the details of life alongside Ratko. They had wanted to know everything, right back to the early days in Knin. They were interested in how he'd shifted from pro-Federation Communist to rabid Serbian nationalist – "my words, not theirs!" wrote Milan – and they were eager for any details around his big 'crimes': Sarajevo, ethnic cleansing, Srebrenica.

I have to admit, Goran, that I pretty much sang like a canary. I didn't see any reason not to. After he told that lie to the head teacher from Srebrenica, any last vestiges of respect or admiration for him went up in smoke. And as I'd been pretty much office-bound due to my role, I didn't see any risk that I'd get the book thrown at me.

Milan said that he was pretty sure that Mick's introduction to the security services in London had saved him from a spell perhaps in a prison cell initially, and certainly a period in a refugee hostel while his case was being considered.

Instead, they stuck me in a characterful tenement flat behind Victoria Street, just a stone's throw from Westminster Abbey, and gave me a security services contact who I could pick the phone up to any time I remembered an additional detail or needed anything. And there I was, a Serbian with not much English, shopping at Safeway and catering for myself for the first time in my life, drifting round the streets of one of the finest capital cities in the world, watching the Grenadier Guards with their bearskin hats and brass instruments as they carried out the Changing of the Guard. After what I'd been through in Croatia and Bosnia, it just seemed surreal.

He had enrolled in free English evening classes provided by the local education authority, and, because he didn't have much else to do, he learned quickly.

The added incentive was that there are fabulous bookshops here, so the quicker I could learn, the quicker I could get onto reading great English and American literature in the original.

But it hadn't all been plain sailing.

There are days when I feel very lonely. I'm a bit nervous about tracking down any 'Serbians in London' groups because you never know what kind of political views individuals might hold – and I certainly don't want to be quizzed about my recent past. So I just knuckle down, go for long walks, and try to keep my mind off the difficult stuff.

Milan said his great breakthrough came when he was given clearance by the Home Office to remain in Britain on the basis that his life could be at risk should he return to Belgrade. He was then able to visit a London college and sit an educational assessment.

They said that, once my English is a little more polished, because of the quality of my Serbian education I'm quite capable of going to university. Now I'm just waiting for the next round of applications and then I'll put in to do a degree in modern history or English literature. Or both. I never spent any money while I was in the army, so I've got quite a lot of savings behind me. Plus, my dad says he'll sub me if I need it.

Which reminds me, Goran: I've been meaning to suggest this for some time, but you really must fix up to meet my dad in Belgrade. I think you two would get along great. You share the same political views. He'll also be able to keep you up to speed on the gossip about Ratko and The Hague and when, if ever, he might get hauled before the tribunal.

Milan said that Goran was probably aware that his father's newspaper, *Borba*, after surviving the outbreak of the wars against all the odds without being shut down, had finally been taken over by the Government in 1994. Milan's father and over a hundred other employees had quit and were soon publishing the same anti-war journalism that had characterised *Borba* under the title of *Naša Borba* ('Our Struggle'). After the war, the same group had gone on to found a new paper, *Danas* ('Today') – a vehicle for left-oriented, social democratic, pro-EU-integration views.

Milan said that Goran should expect a call from his dad, as he would pass on Goran's phone number when he next spoke to him. Then he signed off with a flourish that Goran found heart-warming.

Goran, I'll sign off now, but not before I thank you again for helping me as I began my flight from home. I think of you often, and, though I didn't really know her, I think of Ana often too. I struggle to imagine how you deal with your grief, but I hope you are finding a way through it all.

I sense that, alongside our friendship, we are both now united in wanting to see justice done in relation to Ratko. You lost your life partner due to his actions and I lost my homeland. For me that loss might be temporary. I realise yours is a life sentence, and I wish you the strength and the fortitude you will need to carry you through.

If ever you are able to get away and would like to visit England, do let me know. I can put you up for as long as you want. These days I'm even capable of showing you the sights!

Be strong, be safe, and be sure I'm thinking of you and wishing you well.

Best regards,
Your friend,
Milan

Goran read the letter through twice, then folded it and laid it on the table in front of him. He sat silently for a while. It was a superb letter that had touched him profoundly. Just one detail had jarred with him. Milan had written authoritatively, 'You lost your life partner due to his actions', unaware of the ultimatum he, Goran, had given to Ana. It was conceivable that he had lost his life partner due to his *own* actions. And he didn't need to remind himself that no one would ever know that… unless he told someone.

17

Despite one quick visit to assess his aptitude for the opportunity, Goran hadn't known what to expect when he had made the decision to trade life in Belgrade for a career in Tuzla. But when he landed in Bosnia's third city, moved into a city-centre flat, and began to find his bearings, he sensed an authenticity about its character and he felt he was in a place that was confident in its status. *There is work to be done in this community,* Tuzla seemed to say, *and it will be done in a spirit of cooperation. Meritocracy will trump clan, class or ethnicity. Humanity and endeavour will prevail.*

Tuzla's resistance to the forces of division had been rocked late in the wars when a Bosnian Serb Army shell hit a café in the middle of town. The nature of the missile – a high-explosive fragmentation shell – meant the casualties were high: seventy-one killed and 240 wounded. The fact that all were civilians and many were twenty-five years of age or younger could have led to a sense of demoralisation, but it produced defiance instead. Four years later, as Goran was settling into the town, the massacre's anniversary was marked but Tuzla insisted on continuing to go about its business. President Milošević was engaged in fresh strife in Kosovo, but this was not Tuzla's business.

Goran was based in Tuzla centre but the heartbeat of his work was soon resounding from the villages and hamlets of the region. This city boy was now greedily devouring the mountains, forests and valleys of central Bosnia. For the first time he sensed that he was drawn more instinctively to the rural than a lifelong Belgrade citizen might have imagined he could be.

He didn't kid himself that this rural life held much that was idyllic apart from its frequent stunning views and its clean, cool air. The fathers whose children he tended had weather-beaten faces and hands roughened by the kind of work with which a man like Goran was unacquainted. Escaping poverty was a real challenge. Yet this did not feel like territory alien to him.

His 'clients' treated him with the awe that the untrained feel towards a medical man's apparently magical insights and treatments. It was a respect that he felt elevated him in their eyes to the extent that they would never see him as an equal member of their community; yet he felt that this was his space too. He was made welcome, but he had to strive not to feel like an interloper. Perhaps he was being oversensitive but he felt as though he was feeding off their environment almost without their permission; that they didn't register the spiritual lift he received from the succour he brought to his patients. Each degree of success felt like a privilege granted.

Social workers and nurses, who had earlier reconnoitred the area to try to ensure that no children were neglected or abused and that each child had educational and personal development possibilities, would drive him out to remote areas and he would be expected to know instinctively how to address the problems. He soon realised that the demands upon him were as much about the children's mental state as they were about their physical well-being.

If at times he felt unqualified for the work he was being asked to carry out, he soon came to appreciate that this was precisely the kind of care he had imagined he would be drawn to when he had first realised he had medical ambitions: trying to fix people in need of 'fixing' with pills and potions, but with tenderness, compassion and a little creative psychology as well.

The days were long, the pressure on him was significant, and although, when he retired to his flat at the end of a long day, he was inevitably shutting the door only on himself with no friend or colleague to support him, he felt a satisfying exhaustion.

"This is real work," he heard himself say, as he closed the front door, a few weeks into his role.

He had met Milan's father just before he had moved permanently to Tuzla, and Mr Tešević had nodded approvingly when Goran had told him the nature of the role he would be assuming. It was as if he were saying, *That will be real work.*

Milan's father oozed an earnestness born of a spirit convinced that he was doing serious work too. The fact that he and his journalistic colleagues were trying to hold to account notorious, ruthless leaders like Slobodan Milošević meant that his earnestness had to be married with enormous bravery, but his was a quiet demeanour. Those who attempted to be guardians of the truth tended to be unflashy, but Goran sensed that Mr Tešević's sobriety would not be without a degree of dry humour.

Most satisfying from his introduction to Mr Tešević was the glimpse that Goran sensed he was being offered into the serious, profound man that his son would become – but one endowed above all with true generosity. Another reassuring factor was Mr Tešević's absolute conviction that Milošević would fall and, most likely, that Mladić would fall with him.

"The people at the top of the tree will soon tire of protecting Milošević. The West may not have covered itself in glory in Yugoslavia over this past decade, but they'll gradually tighten the sanctions noose or erect obstacles to Serbia joining the liberal, democratic club of nations until any loyalty to Slobo is squeezed out," he told Goran.

"So you think they'll both end up in The Hague, then?" asked Goran.

"Yes, I do. It's tough for people like us to be patient but, without wanting to sound pompous or portentous, their deeds will catch up with them. I've little doubt about that."

Thinking back from Tuzla on their initial exchanges, Goran recalled Mr Tešević's most striking physical feature: his impressive salt-and-pepper 'weave'. Like a stretch of forest on a distant hilltop, it was no toupée but natural hair that was neither straight nor curly. Goran struggled to imagine what effect a comb might have on it, and he sensed a barber might have to trim it like hedging rather than scissor-cut it in any orthodox way. Together with his keen, dark eyes, it gave Milan's father an air of distinction.

But Goran realised that he was recalling Mr Tešević at that moment because of the spiritual contrast he represented to the colleagues Goran increasingly spent time with. Goran and Milan's father had quickly settled on shared agnostic – if not atheistic – territory in their conversation. They hadn't felt the need to make anything of it; it was simply a mooring of their contextual terrain, an acknowledgement that their beliefs had adjacent cartographic coordinates. But now Goran's colleagues were Christians from World Vision from a range of backgrounds – from Catholic to Methodist to Serbian Orthodox – or they were Bosnian Muslims. Not one of these colleagues sought to proselytise or imply that theirs might be a superior belief system, but Goran was noticing increasingly that these people, who not only had a faith but had volunteered to pursue careers in support of others rather than in pursuit of wealth, had a calmness and a selflessness that he admired. He hoped he had reached his own calm selflessness via the gifts of sound upbringing and rationality. But the thought came at him until he was obliged to concede that there may be something to it: was there something about their version that set it apart from his? He thought of it as scaling the same peak, using two different trails – but the sense that theirs might represent a more satisfying journey than his nagged away at him. From the sidelines he occasionally observed their rituals – kissing icons, or a Muslim's daily prayers – and he had no desire to participate, but at times he was in awe of the spell their belief seemed to cast. Why was it that he felt many of them were more fulfilling company than the average layperson? How was it that they appeared capable of deepening his job satisfaction? Was it because there appeared to be a seamlessness between their spirits and their actions?

But there they were again: these heavy questions; these huge issues. Since he had first met Ana and understood her situation, these questions hadn't so much multiplied as become relentless; they had come in wave after wave. He had no peace. He endeavoured to park them, but they just kept returning.

"It's because things matter to you, Goran. You've always wanted to do good, to do the best you can, to understand everything around you. Even as a young child you could never accept injustice," his mother had told him recently, when he had asked her how he might reach a place of peace and stop worrying about every last detail of the human – or might it be divine? – condition. "I'm not sure you'll ever stop questioning and fighting for what's right – but that's good, Goran. Your dad and I respect you for it. It might be a price worth paying."

He had shrugged at that last comment before conceding that his mother might be right.

He recalled too Ana remarking that he had integrity that lacked an off-switch. He had taken it as a compliment, but he sensed that she was saying to him that it was okay sometimes to drift into neutral. One didn't have to be on full moral alert one hundred per cent of the time. But then the question became just too big again. If integrity was a frame of mind, how could you turn it off? He didn't challenge her. He just let the comment drift.

But perhaps now, if he immersed himself in trying to put these broken Bosnian children back together again, the sheer mental and physical exhaustion might crowd out the questions. He hoped they might. He wasn't convinced they would.

If Goran's own loss was far from trivial, there was an immediacy about the traumas of some of the children he met that was capable of temporarily blotting out his past and stilling the endless questioning. One of the social workers he sometimes helped as he travelled round the Tuzla region had asked him to accompany her to a small settlement called Čaklovići Gornji, about ten kilometres east of the city.

Selveta was a Muslim, not far off thirty years of age, he guessed, with frizzy dark brown hair tied back in a bun, plain clear features, and dark brown eyes that sparkled anywhere where there was the slightest chink of light. When he had worked alongside her in the past, he had been struck by her quiet, confident manner and uncanny ability to communicate, sometimes without need for words, with children who often sought refuge from their trauma or their poverty in silence.

The boy they were visiting on this occasion was eleven years of age and had been traumatised by the experience of making one of his regular trips on foot to his grandfather's house just a few hundred yards from the family home, only to find that JNA officers had slit his grandfather's throat in a revenge attack for the killing of many of their colleagues in an ambush by Bosnia's Territorial Defence Force. Several years on, the boy was far from a full recovery, shrinking into a world of his own and barely speaking. Selveta wanted Goran to examine him and assess whether he was suffering from malnutrition, while she continued her mission to try to coax the boy back into some kind of communal space.

"His parents are simple people who work the land. I'm not being patronising but they haven't got the emotional range to help bring him out of himself," Selveta said. She explained that he loved to draw, but that for some years now his sketches had featured prone figures with pools of blood issuing from their heads, or bombs falling on frightened villagers. He was not alone among his peers in this, but he was proving among the most difficult to set on the road to recovery.

The boy's parents nodded respectfully as Goran stepped into their humble wooden homestead on the fringes of a tiny hamlet that he estimated would house just a couple of hundred people. Although he was recently qualified, he sensed that they were in awe of his training and status, and he was already learning that in these remote parts it was better not to try to reorder that relationship. Selveta had told him that there might be occasions on which they might need to remove a child for treatment or care, and enjoying that status and trust and the authority that went with them might make all the difference between rescuing a child or not.

There was no doubt that the boy was a little underweight and could do with bulking up, but this was not a case of malnutrition. Goran guessed that there would be sufficient vegetables and the odd cut of lamb available in the environs to make sure he didn't go hungry.

"Are you able to feed him lamb and vegetables regularly?" he asked the boy's mother.

"Oh, yes, he doesn't go short, Doctor. It's just that he doesn't always have an appetite for everything on his plate... and I don't like to force him."

Goran laid a hand on the shoulder of this frail, brown-eyed boy and said, "Now, Elvedin, I need you to do your best and eat up all your meals. You need to get stronger, and we don't want your mum worrying about you, do we?"

The boy shook his head vigorously but didn't reply.

"So will you do that for me? Eat up your meals?"

Elvedin nodded. Goran hoped he saw the edges of a smile form, but the moment was gone and his serious face reset.

"Good lad," said Goran. "I'll come back and see you in a couple of weeks. See if you can't have finished all your meals by then, eh?"

"Okay," said Selveta. "Shall we go for our walk?"

Elvedin nodded, and Selveta took his hand. She jerked her head to make clear that Goran was to come with her and the boy.

Outside, the three of them walked to the top of the street and then climbed a stile into a meadow offering views across the hillsides around.

"Right. So, shall we sing a song?"

Elvedin looked up at Selveta. "You sing," he said quietly.

"Well, I'll start and then you can join in. Okay?"

He nodded, and this time he did smile shyly.

"And which song shall we sing?" asked Selveta.

Goran was sensing that this was the ritual each time she visited Elvedin, and he could feel the atmosphere of calm she was spinning around him. If Elvedin's parents were in awe of him, Goran, he was already in awe of Selveta's natural, social fluency with this child.

"The one about the mountain," Elvedin said.

"Okay – 'How Big is Jahora's Mountain?' I'll start and then you join in."

Goran had heard the song before – played almost like a hornpipe, at a fair lick, with a rollicking accordion accompaniment – but as soon as Selveta began to sing, he realised hers would have a hymnic quality to it.

Oh, how big is Jahora's mountain? How big is Jahora's mountain?

Goran was taken aback by the sweetness and the quality of Selveta's voice. She picked out her notes with the confidence of someone used to performing in public, and projected as far as the birds in the trees. Elvedin continued to hold Selveta's hand. He didn't join in the song, but he gazed up at her as if bewitched. After just two sentences of the song's lyrics, Goran understood that the boy would look forward to the visits of this songstress eagerly, yearning for the next visit from the moment the notes of the last song melted into the breeze.

Oh, the grey falcon cannot fly over it, the grey falcon cannot fly over it,
Let alone a great hero on a horse, let alone a great hero on a horse.

But the young girl ran over it without a horse, the young girl ran over it without a horse.

Oh, all Bosnian men saddle good horses, all Bosnian men saddle good horses.

And Bosnian women comb their red hair, Bosnian women comb their red hair.

Goran couldn't help himself from bursting into applause, his heart warming as a smile of joy overcame Elvedin's face. "Oh, Selveta sings so beautifully, doesn't she, Elvedin?" he said excitedly.

Elvedin nodded again, the smile this time taking some time to leach from his face.

"Thank you, thank you!" Selveta said. "Now let's do it again, but you, Elvedin, and you, Goran, join in too."

Goran joined in as best he could, conscious that he was no vocalist. Beneath Selveta's equally impressive reprise, he could just hear the softest of notes coming from Elvedin.

There were more songs, and there were horses in fields and tethered goats to encounter before they headed back to the homestead. For a quiet boy, largely mute in the company of his parents, Goran could only guess at the scale of the thrill Elvedin would derive from these visits.

Before Goran stepped out of the house to rejoin Selveta, who had set out to start the car, Elvedin's mother touched him on the arm.

"Oh, Doctor, thank you so much for what you have done."

"Well, thank you – but my role was nothing compared to Selveta's."

"Doctor, you can't imagine how much it lifts him. Even if he doesn't say much, I know he's uplifted. He said to me once – just once – 'Oh, Mum, when she sings, I think she's an angel.' If you can keep coming…" Her voice tailed away, and some of the sadness Goran had sensed initially returned.

"Don't worry – I'm sure Selveta will keep up her visits."

In the car on the way back to Tuzla, Selveta explained that her aim was gradually to convince Elvedin that no one was going to come and kill his father as they had killed his grandfather, and that no more bombs were going to fall on their villages. "Sometimes I say it explicitly, and other times I just talk to the animals with him, look at the pear trees, and try to enjoy the landscape and the views. It's a slow process but I'm edging him bit by bit back into the world beyond his internal world. It breaks my heart sometimes to see how shrunken within himself he's become – but that's why I have to keep coming back."

"Well, that's some singing voice you've got. He obviously loves that. Where did you get a voice like that from?"

"Oh, we're all musical in my family. Before and during the bad days, that's how we'd pass the time. My dad would play the saz, my grandfather would play the accordion before he died, and we'd play all the best *Sevdalinka* songs – especially the sad ones."

Even as a citizen of Belgrade, Goran was conscious of *Sevdalinka* music: traditional melancholic Bosnian folk songs, often accompanied by a long-necked lute called a saz.

If the experience of hearing Selveta sing to Elvedin and observing her conjuring the boy back towards some kind of normality made this a special day, it was merely at the top end of a spectrum containing enormous challenges and profound satisfaction at even the most modest improvements to the damaged lives of the Tuzla region's children.

But there was a different kind of fillip a couple of evenings later, when the phone rang in Goran's flat. Not very many people had his new phone number but, when he answered, he heard the voice not of one of his parents, but of Milan's father.

"Goran, it's Danijel Tešević here; Milan's dad."

"Oh, hi, Mr Tešević. Good to hear from you." Goran masked his surprise at Mr Tešević's initiative in calling him.

"I thought you'd like to know before the general public. They've got Slobo. They've lifted him."

"Really?!"

"Yes – he's finally off to The Hague. The tribunal might be a worthwhile operation after all."

Both Goran and Milan's father had been surprised when, having lost elections in September 2000, Milošević's Special Forces had not intervened to overturn the results by force, but perhaps they had concluded that, as sanctions bit harder and harder and a loose student resistance movement, Otpor, began to spread across Serbia, the writing was on the wall – literally. When Goran had last been in Belgrade, the Otpor logo of a clenched fist and the words 'Gotov je!' ('He's finished!') were stencilled everywhere. There had been a six-month stand-off post elections as Milošević was spared incarceration, but eventually he was arrested and taken to Belgrade Central Prison on charges of financial irregularity.

"This was always just a stopgap, Goran," said Mr Tešević. "Everybody in the new Government knew Serbia and Yugoslavia's hopes of raising big international funding to rebuild were dependent on Slobo being carted off to The Hague on much more serious charges. There's a donors' conference in a couple of days' time and they're looking for a billion dollars. The US won't chip in unless he's behind bars in the Netherlands. That's what finally persuaded the Government to lift the constitutional block on extradition."

"And what about Ratko? Doesn't the same logic apply to him?" asked Goran.

"Well, there's a bit of bad news there. My sources tell me that the West was offered a two-for-one deal by our Prime Minister. The CIA's station chief and MI6's top official in Belgrade were supplied with the address where Ratko's allegedly hiding, but the deal was they had to send their own soldiers to arrest him. Turns out neither the Americans nor the British were prepared to dispatch elite forces to Serbia at such short notice on the basis of an unconfirmed tip. To be fair, the SAS or the CIA would have been flying out into a dangerous situation without being sure about their chances of success," said Mr Tešević. "So he lives to tell the tale."

"The bastard," said Goran.

"But don't worry, Goran. He'll get his come-uppance. It just might take a bit more time."

After hanging up, Goran felt slightly flat. He trusted Danijel Tešević's judgement. His forecasts had been accurate so far, but how good would it have been to have celebrated a double lift of Slobo and Ratko with a beer in downtown Tuzla – even if he would have been drinking alone?

He picked up the large framed photograph of Ana that he kept permanently on the sideboard and kissed it. He wondered what Ana might be thinking now, had she had a consciousness beyond the grave of what had happened and what had not happened today. He wasn't receiving any radio waves from her for the moment.

A few days later Goran attended a musical evening at the home of Selveta's parents in a district of Tuzla known as the artistic quarter. Selveta had invited a few colleagues but he had the sense that she had arranged the evening largely for him because she was aware of his relative isolation far from his home and his friends in Belgrade. Given her daily professional and emotional commitments, it was a kind gesture, if his hunch was correct.

Selveta's father played the saz, a neighbour played the accordion, and of course, Selveta sang. If he had one long-term regret in his life, Goran rued not having learned a musical instrument and therefore not experienced the thrill of playing with friends and family in a band. However, during the highlight of Selveta's outstanding vocal performance that evening – *'Pijana sam i bez pića'* ('I am Drunk but Not with Wine') – his heart was fit to burst at the vicarious high he experienced at this shared musical ecstasy. His life, shut down so violently by Ana's death, was gradually expanding into the space around him and, he felt, deepening in value now that he had knowledge and caring to dispense and was operating alongside some exceptional people.

18

About a month later, Selveta dropped by to finalise arrangements for a visit that she and Goran would make together the following day. It was the first time that she had been to his flat.

He put coffee on and was digging out some biscuits when he became aware of Selveta being drawn to the sideboard by the photograph of Ana upon it. Because he rarely had visitors, and because he was so used to the picture and its location, he had stopped thinking of the effect it might have on anyone who stepped into the flat. Because of the angle at which the photograph had been taken, Ana's gaze appeared to be seeking out eye contact with any and every visitor. The photo featured her with Goran's favourite elf-like haircut. He never ceased to thrill at her bright eyes and watermelon smile in that picture, however many times he looked at it. Selveta, who had been chatting about work arrangements, fell silent as she took in the details of the photograph at close quarters. He had been aware of her walking to it and then placing her hands on either side of the frame. Goran didn't fill the silence. He did wonder whether he should have positioned the picture in a less conspicuous place.

"Goran?" asked Selveta. "I hope I'm not being nosy, but is this your girlfriend back in Belgrade? She's really beautiful."

He could sense that she had been taken aback. He had never spoken about a girlfriend, and of course, he had never talked to Selveta or anyone in Tuzla about his loss.

"She *was* my girlfriend…"

"Oh, I'm sorry. Did you have to split when you came here?"

Goran paused. He had to decide in an instant how much to divulge. "No… She died… In fact, worse than that: she killed herself."

Selveta held a hand to her mouth in shock. "Oh, Goran, I'm so, so sorry. I really shouldn't have asked." She laid a hand on his forearm. "Forgive me, forgive me."

"No, don't worry, Selveta. It's okay."

Selveta appeared on the verge of panic, convinced that she had committed a serious social gaffe. "Stupid me!" she chided herself. "I'm so used to trying to figure out other people's lives at work, I can't switch off the personal questions outside of work." She touched his forearm again. "I'm sorry – I'm so, so sorry."

"Really, really, Selveta. It's okay. I would have told you anyway… sometime… soon." He paused. "It's just, it's not a great conversation opener, is it?" And he raised his eyebrows at the self-evident nature of his comment. "Let me fetch us some coffee."

Goran was still figuring out in his mind just how far to go. Be light on details, leave it sketchy – or give her the full story? Or a version that stopped short of making the Ratko Mladić link? As a Muslim, might she be appalled by the Mladić connection? Might it affect their relationship – professional or personal? Or both? Well, it was certain to – but would it be terminal?

Goran had beckoned Selveta to sit down opposite him on his two-seater sofa. He placed her cup in the saucer in front of her with the precision of a Grandmaster placing a chess piece onto a killer square, so anxious was he not to spill coffee from the cup in his state of confusion. The situation somehow reminded him of the time when Milan had recounted his tale of desertion from the sofa in Goran's Belgrade flat, though then the focus had been on Milan. Now Goran was in the spotlight.

He looked purposefully into Selveta's eyes. "She was a medical student with me at the Faculty at Belgrade University. We started at the same time and we struck up pretty soon after we started our studies. She was called Ana, and we had plans to work together – maybe at first in Africa, or perhaps somewhere like here. I thought we were life partners."

Goran was tempted to stop there. He doubted Selveta would quiz him further, given her reaction to what she saw as her initial faux pas, but some instinct within him told him it might be helpful to share. Without the understanding of Selveta that he had acquired over weeks and months, he suspected that he would have kept it vague. But when he thought back over their exchanges after the event, he knew that he had sensed without fully articulating the thought internally that this might be the character with the empathy and the subtlety most suited to deal with the enormity of his revelation.

"Thing was, I didn't know it at first," said Goran, lowering his gaze, "but her father was a military man. A Bosnian Serb. And when the wars broke out, nobody knew him, but then he rose through the ranks and…" Goran paused. "This is the difficult bit… We think he was responsible for multiple killings… maybe even genocide."

The alarm on Selveta's face was everything Goran had expected. It was as if she were holding her breath.

"And in the end, Ana just couldn't take it. She was planning to swear the Hippocratic oath and her dad was, if not a mass murderer, responsible for ordering mass murder." He paused again. He realised he needed to swallow in order to continue. "She wouldn't talk to me about it, Selveta. Not at all, though sometimes I raised the bigger issue about the wars; about their justification. But no – not a word… And then I found her dead in her flat. She couldn't take the ignominy any more."

Selveta put her hands over her mouth in horror. A tear plinked down onto the table by her coffee cup, then another. "Oh, my God!" she whispered. "So did she overdose?"

"No – worse than that. She shot herself… Shot herself with her dad's pistol. It was lying there on the floor when I let myself into her flat."

Selveta clapped her hands over her eyes and began to sob deeply. Goran felt tears well up in his eyes too, but he tried not to let them fall or allow a vale of tears to break.

Selveta stood up and walked round to his chair before crouching down and gripping his hand. Her brown eyes sparkled all the more from the film of tears upon them. "Oh, Goran! I'm so, so sorry. I had no idea you were carrying so much pain. And I'm so sorry if I made you tell me."

Goran had taken control over his own tears. He wouldn't sob. His feeling was now one of relief at having found someone with the capacity to take on board his story and respond appropriately. "You didn't make me tell you, Selveta. I would have told you… when the time was right." He paused. "And today, the time was right." He had gone as far as he needed to go at this stage. He *would* tell her that his girlfriend had been Ana Mladić whose father was wanted for genocide at The Hague Tribunal but was still on the run. Just not now.

Which was the correct call, because the following day, as Selveta nudged her car into another remote village, she said, "Goran, you don't need to answer this, and if you don't I promise I'll never ask you again, but I've been thinking about it and I was wondering: was Ana the daughter of Ratko Mladić?"

Goran left a respectful pause. "Yes, Selveta. Yes, I'm afraid she was."

Selveta had reached their destination. She pulled on the handbrake and switched off the engine. She looked across at him. He was wondering whether he might be subject to an accusatory gaze – for being associated with a man responsible for the killing of tens of thousands of her Muslim brothers. But instead, there was only compassion.

And she said it again. "Goran, I'm so, so sorry." And she laid her right hand on his left.

He began to justify himself. "When I first met her, there was no war and he was just away a lot as a professional soldier. I had no idea that..." He paused again. "And then I was so smitten with Ana... Well, what could I do? Walk away? Selveta, I just couldn't."

She patted his hand. "Goran, you've got nothing to apologise for. Nor has Ana. You're not responsible for anyone else's actions. I just hate to think of the suffering you've been through."

"And you don't hate me for tolerating an association with a man most likely guilty of genocide?"

"Hate you?!" Selveta looked almost affronted by the question. "Heavens, Goran, I'll *never* hate you. You're a decent, compassionate man. You are in no way tainted by the stain of Ratko Mladić."

"Thank you, Selveta. Thank you." He looked out of the passenger-side window at nothing in particular and then he said, "You know, Selveta, I wonder sometimes whether what I'm doing here is some kind of reparation to the people who bore the brunt of the violence. Violence inflicted mainly by Serbs and Bosnian Serbs on other Bosnians."

"Well, that's noble, if it's the case. And even if it isn't, the work you're doing is noble. We Bosnians appreciate it." She unclicked her door. "Come on – work to do."

In the days and weeks that followed, Goran had three main reflections. First, a strong sense of relief that he had been able to reveal his secret to Selveta. He hadn't asked her not to share his revelation with other colleagues but it would have been out of character for her to have done so. He would have dealt with others being aware of the Mladić connection but it was better that it lay solely with discreet Selveta at this stage.

His second reflection was that he still felt some shame at not having shared with Selveta the detail that he had given Ana an ultimatum. He had told Selveta he couldn't leave her, yet the truth was that, on the day before her death, he had told Ana he *would* leave her – though he had never expected that he would need to. He had expected her to choose him ahead of her father. Yet he was still the only extant person who knew about the ultimatum and he wasn't yet ready to tell anyone about it. If he felt a little shame – here, now, with Selveta – perhaps this was a rare occasion on which he could allow himself the privilege of reaching for the one hundred per cent integrity off-switch.

The third reflection related to his relationship with Selveta. He didn't think he was overanalysing the situation but, for a few seconds after Selveta had spotted Ana's picture and before she had asked who it was, he had sensed that she might have been not just shocked but perhaps disappointed to discover that he was 'spoken for'. Had she harboured romantic ambitions? He hadn't detected them before, though they worked well together, but on reflection, he now believed he had detected a little pang of disappointment being rapidly suppressed within her. However, in a heartbeat he had gone from being spoken for to being a figure tragically stripped of his life partner. And the truth was that that big photograph of Ana in his flat, that story of loss and blood, had made him even more unavailable in Selveta's eyes than he had been when she had thought he had a beautiful girlfriend back in Belgrade. They were nowhere near talking about this but he sensed that she would think it unseemly were she to make a move for him, having heard his story. And the emotional consequence of that was that she would think it unseemly were he to make a move for her. He wasn't ready for that in any case, but external events beyond their control had slapped a huge 'no-go' zone onto the landscape of their relationship.

The months turned into years and Goran began to feel that the World Vision team, social workers, and doctors like himself were beginning to turn a corner in the Tuzla region. Selveta's forensic scouting for children at risk or in need, allied with her outstanding organisational skills and profound emotional intelligence, meant that she was central to the improvements to the situation.

Goran and Selveta grew closer to the extent that they began to know intuitively what each other was thinking, but the platonic pall that had been cast over them by Selveta's discovery of Ana's story remained in place. At times Goran felt that he would like to lift it but, at crunch moments, he would step back, gripped by a sense that he had unfinished business. He knew Selveta wouldn't take the first step out of respect for Ana.

But when Goran was approached by a hospital in Sarajevo and asked to lead a department in its paediatric service, he knew he could only take on the job if Selveta would agree to come to the capital too and play a central role in the work of the unit. He had begun his professional career with her alongside him. She had been key to his appreciating the challenges he faced, and now he could barely conceive of stepping into a more senior role without the security her guidance and insights would provide him with. But it wasn't just about him: he believed she would be a formidable unit organiser and counsellor. Fortunately for him, she agreed. He could tell that leaving her family in Tuzla would be a wrench for her, but he sensed too that she was ready for promotion and for greater responsibility in a new context.

They moved into flats just half a kilometre apart in the Baščaršija area. Post siege, Sarajevo had reacquired its cosmopolitan flavour, but Baščaršija was the district most favoured by the capital's Muslims. But before they had settled in properly, news broke that Slobodan Milošević had died. Goran had watched clips of his trial in The Hague on TV in disgust as the former Serbian and Yugoslav President had turned his trial into a circus, firing his legal team, running his own defence case, and submitting witnesses to as much humiliation, scorn and insult as he could muster. If his fierce intellect shone through, so did his moral vacuity.

"You loathsome man," Goran had heard himself mutter at the TV after one particularly hubristic session.

Milan's father was soon on the phone to Goran with the inside track on a demise that robbed prosecutors of the chance to convict Milošević and jail him – most likely for life. "He couldn't bear being separated from his wife, Mira. They'd been high-school sweethearts. Inseparable. She'd quit Serbia for Moscow in 2003. She was afraid the authorities might come after her if she stayed in Belgrade. Slobo then kept trying to be sent to Moscow for treatment for his heart condition but, when they wouldn't let him leave The Hague, he just stopped taking his blood pressure pills and other pills to counter the effects of the blood pressure. He effectively killed himself," said Danijel.

Were Ratko to stop taking the drugs that Milan had sought for him on that Belgrade visit, he would go the same way, Goran reflected ruefully.

The Milošević episode upset him. Not only were liberals and peace activists robbed of Slobo being convicted; Ratko was not even behind bars in The Hague. The trail had gone cold – in part because Mladić had had to go deep underground, unable to drop into select Belgrade events and thumb his nose at the authorities once the Serbian Government had handed in Milošević.

Goran was setting up his new flat and taking his possessions out of boxes when Selveta popped in.

"Fucking Milošević, eh?" Goran said. "Excuse my French but the bastard couldn't even face the music, could he?" And he shook his head in frustration.

"Yes – bad, isn't it?" said Selveta.

Goran regretted his bad language. He didn't use it in front of Selveta generally and he sensed she wasn't comfortable with it, but his anger had got the better of him. Goran lifted the framed photo of Ana out of one of the packing boxes and stood it up on a sideboard. If the location wasn't quite so centre stage as it had been in his Tuzla flat, the photograph would still be prominent; hard for a visitor to overlook.

Selveta spoke softly. "Goran, it's not really my business, but at some point you need to put away that photo. Keep it near by all means, but put it away."

Goran was stunned into silence and looked at Selveta in pure shock.

"I'm not saying you need to move on, Goran, but…" She paused as if she'd crafted a thought and articulated it without knowing where it was leading. "Well, actually, maybe I *am* saying you need to move on."

Goran didn't touch the picture. It remained on the sideboard where he had placed it, but he sat down in an armchair, locked his fingers together in his lap, and gazed ahead of himself without focusing on any item. "Selveta, this Milošević business has got to me. It's like he's wriggled free." He reflected silently for a moment. "It's just I can't sit back and relax until they've got Ratko. He mustn't escape." He looked up at Selveta. "Once they've got him, that's my task over. That man effectively destroyed my Ana and he's not going to get away with it. I won't rest till he's caught."

Selveta crouched down by the arm of his chair. He realised that she had a disarming way of lowering her voice to just above a whisper when she had a delicate point to make. "Goran, you mustn't let that man poison your well. I know he's destroyed your life plan with Ana but don't let him destroy your life too. You're doing *so* much good for others here. Step back and be kind to yourself." She paused before delivering her final, daring point. "Ana would have wanted that… wouldn't she?"

Goran's eyes welled with tears and he gave a little sob, before putting his hand to his mouth and gradually composing himself. Selveta patted his forearm gently, then squeezed his hand.

A couple of days later, Goran called Milan. They shared dismay at Milošević's "shuffling free", as Goran put it, and agreed it was high time Ratko was brought to book.

"Anyway, Milan, that's not why I rang. I'm starting a new job in Sarajevo shortly but I've got time for a break. I could fly to England to meet you, if you can squeeze me in."

A week later Goran was dropped by taxi at the front door of a semi-detached house in Torquay. He had never been to England before. The street that Milan lived in typified for Goran a neatness and an orderliness about English urban life that he had read about and seen pictures of but had never believed to be such a central feature. They weren't, as he had expected, a few examples photographed for their uniqueness. These streets of semi-detached houses with trim little front gardens were everywhere. That his friend had landed here from the grandeur and grit of Belgrade he found difficult to compute. The scale of Milan's transition in just over a decade was close to bewildering.

He and Milan had corresponded and had had the occasional phone call over the years, to an extent that Goran felt he had kept track of his friend's personal and professional trajectory. But as he waited for the front door to open, he felt a degree of nervousness. He had no reason to expect their catch-up and reacquaintance to be anything other than straightforward and satisfying. He expected their bond to be faster after they had shared details of the journeys they had each been on since they had last met; yet he knew that his decision to share with Milan in the course of his visit a detail he had shared with no one else would gnaw away, like a hamster lodged in the pit of his stomach, until his revelation was out. He didn't doubt the need for the revelation, he didn't think Milan would react with anything but understanding, but it put a temporary check on any unalloyed enjoyment of their reunion.

Milan came to the door, still sallow, still slim, but having acquired a maturity of demeanour that the youthful Milan had lacked when Goran had first lighted upon him on the Mladićs' lawn all those years ago. If he wasn't quite close in aspect to the gravitas of his father with his serious air and salt-and-pepper hair, Milan's baby face had acquired lines; his blue eyes, bordering on grey, had acquired an air of deepening wisdom. Instantly Goran felt a surge of love for this man. Yes – Milan was on a journey that would take him closer to the man of admirable integrity that was his father than to the youngster captivated by the reputation and leadership skills of Ratko Mladić, but, simply from the glow he exuded, Goran could see straight away that Milan's route to the light was irreversible; complete.

Goran was ushered in after a bear hug between the two young men on the doorstep, his first duty to meet Milan's partner, Sandra. He had been alerted in advance by Milan that he had settled down with an English woman. Goran warmed to her straight away. If she was plain, her face spoke unmistakably of generosity and kindness. She had wavy shoulder-length hair that stopped just on the blonde side of strawberry blonde. She was wearing a Snoopy sweatshirt and sky-blue jeans. Milan would tell Goran later that, after taking his degree at Exeter University in history and English, he had met Sandra at the school at which he had taken his first job. She taught chemistry and, as Milan described it, after he landed in the staffroom, there seemed to be an inevitability about their drifting together. They were soon to be married.

Milan revealed that, some time ago, he had contacted his friend Mick Morrison from *The Times* and sought his advice about how much he should reveal to Sandra about his hinterland.

"I haven't told her, Mick. I'm afraid of losing her," he had told the journalist who had helped secure his right to stay in Britain.

Mick had said, "Milan, you have to come completely clean with her about the whole story. If you don't, the whole thing can blow up in your face later. You tell her everything – but remember you weren't responsible for Srebrenica. He was. Maybe you say you were a bit starstruck at first, but tell her the story about you deserting; why you deserted. Don't soft-soap it, but don't suggest you were guilty of anything you weren't. If you need me, I'll vouch for you, Milan... But if she knows you, I think she'll understand that you weren't culpable. Naive, maybe, early on – but, hell, who wasn't when they were nineteen? She'll love you, Milan – but only if you're straight... about everything."

Mick had never met Sandra but his instincts were sound. Milan told Goran he had told Sandra his backstory soberly, just at the point when they were to commit to each other. He had warned her that there was an outside chance that the media might come after him. It might embarrass her. Aware of the conservative English family she came from and the potential implications and risks for them, he told her that any publicity might make her and her family regret their association.

She had fallen silent for what seemed like minutes but may have been just thirty seconds. Then she said, "Milan, I know you. I know you and you are a good man. I'm grateful for you telling me. But that makes me more determined to hold on to you... provided you want to hold on to me."

Milan replied, "Sandra, I absolutely want to hold on to you."

There was something blissful about this town that Milan had landed in so extraordinarily. They called this coast the English Riviera. It had palm trees. As Goran strolled along the seafront with Milan and Sandra and a warm breeze came off the sea, he could scarcely believe he was in England. In the years he had spent in central Bosnia, he had come to appreciate that there was little to match the drama of that region's landscapes; yet the clashing contrast with this English coastal town lay in Torquay's affluence and social tranquillity set against the brutal war legacy and the economic devastation of Bosnia. Here was Milan settling comfortably – and deservedly – into his new environment, becoming English effectively, while virtually every young person with potential in Bosnia was looking for an escape route abroad. Milan's hopes were being fulfilled. His hard work was being rewarded. Hope was being choked out of the majority of Bosnia's young people.

For a moment Goran felt a pang of guilt as he strolled in the Torquay sunshine. He had had months and years of largely unrelenting front-line work in the Tuzla region, so any break made him feel as though he was skiving. Then he remembered that he would soon be back in Sarajevo, doing his best to put back together Bosnia's broken children. *You have nothing to apologise for. You're doing your bit*, a voice inside him opined. For once, there was no alternative voice challenging that assertion.

So he allowed himself to relax for a couple of days, as Milan played the perfect local guide and Sandra and Milan provided perfect hospitality. Goran's English was limited but he worked hard to include Sandra in conversations, tried not to marginalise her by slipping too often into Serbian with Milan, and urged Milan to translate when his English was inadequate and he wanted to share a point of conversation that he thought might be of interest to her.

But on day four of his stay Sandra urged them both to leave her to prepare the evening meal. "Milan, take Goran to The Hole in the Wall. He needs to experience it. Have a couple of pints, speak Serbian to your hearts' content, and I'll have food on the table at 7.30pm."

The beamed ceiling and cobbled floor of Torquay's sixteenth-century hostelry were remarkable to a Serbian, the atmosphere everything Goran could have imagined of a traditional English pub, and his first sip of a beer called Brakspear tasted of smoked twigs. It was sensational, in the literal sense of the word. The combination of location, atmosphere and drink almost dissuaded him from his moment of revelation. But, with Sandra out of the conversation, he knew he had to seize the moment or miss it altogether.

Goran had decided that he had to share with someone the fact that he had issued Ana with an ultimatum. He had implied to everyone who had elicited her story from him that it was Ratko who was solely to blame for Ana's death. He now needed to admit that perhaps he was also partially to blame.

For some time, the knowledge that only he knew about the ultimatum was comforting. There could be no retribution from anyone if he told no one. But that felt like a kind of cowardice. Over time, it had begun to drag him down. The secret weighed more and more heavily upon him. Perhaps it was his integrity with no off-switch that was driving him, but he had to get out there a more accurate version of the demise of Ana. He wasn't sure what 'out there' meant. It didn't mean telling the whole world that he shared part of the blame, but how about starting with Milan and taking it from there? He had considered initially sharing the detail with Selveta, but her reaction to learning the story of Ana's death had somehow made her a less appropriate confidante. Her suggestion to him that he needed to 'move on' from Ana made her still less appropriate. He couldn't move on until he had shared this crucial nugget with someone and seen how they would react. In the absence of Selveta, Milan – with his understanding of Ratko and the situation – was the obvious next best confidant, if not quite simply the best confidant, Selveta included.

"Sometimes I go to see Torquay United play. It's not quite Red Star Belgrade but…" Milan laughed.

Goran realised he had not been listening to Milan. "Listen, Milan. There's something I need to share with you." He paused.

Milan registered the fact that Goran's demeanour had slipped abruptly to serious.

"It's just, there's something I've never told anyone else… And I need to get it out… And I think you're the right person to tell."

Milan's brow furrowed at the change in mood. "Whatever. By all means, tell me."

"Well, you know that I said Ana couldn't live with the ignominy of her father's actions? Well… there was another factor." Goran swallowed and knew that Milan could read his distress. "I had been thinking about it for a long time – not just months. A couple of years. I figured that Ana and I were going to have to swear the latest version of the Hippocratic oath once we qualified as doctors. Now, you've no reason to know this, but what we would be swearing – and in fact what I *have* subsequently sworn after Ana's death – is totally incompatible with association with someone guilty of ethnic cleansing, murder or genocide.

"So I bided my time. I knew I would have to do it at some point, but I realised I would have to challenge her and say that she either had to revoke her relationship with her father or we could no longer be a couple. I suppose what I was really saying was that she wouldn't morally be able to swear the Hippocratic oath and mean it if she continued a relationship with him. But I had to force the point."

Milan's eyes bulged and focused sharply on Goran. "Holy shit!" he whispered.

"Milan, I left it till I felt I was in the strongest position. The first Markale market bombing happened and I was convinced that that was her dad's handiwork. But then, as peace initiatives began to roll in – as you told me – he just kept pushing the boundaries, blitzing Bosnian Muslim villages for fear of losing them in any peace deal.

"Milan… the day she killed herself I had finally said to her, 'Ana, you have to choose. Me or him?' I was sure she would choose me…" Tears began to trickle down Goran's cheeks. "What I hadn't imagined was that she had a third option: choosing neither of us, but killing herself instead. And the fact that she used her dad's pistol suggests that she'd framed this third option sometime before my ultimatum."

Milan stretched his arm across the table and placed it on Goran's bicep. "Man… man… That's terrible. Oh, Jesus, that's tragic."

Goran let a few more tears fall before brushing what was left from his face and trying to compose himself. "So, ironic as it may seem, I don't place all the blame for Ana's death at Ratko's door. I was responsible for part of it."

Milan let the words sink in. He left a respectful pause, then said, "I'm not sure that's right, Goran. You didn't order the bombing of the market. You didn't clear those Muslim villages. The shame Ana felt was entirely down to stuff Ratko did or Ratko sanctioned. Don't blame yourself."

"I'm not blaming myself. I did what I did – but what I'm saying to you is, if I hadn't said what I said, told her she had to choose - me or him - mightn't she still be here now?"

Milan thought for a moment. "So are you saying you wish you hadn't given her that ultimatum? I mean, Christ, Goran, that was some dilemma. Challenge her to renounce her father, or ignore it and let things ride."

Goran looked to the side, away from Milan. He took some deep breaths. Then he turned back to Milan and looked him in the eye. "Do you know, Milan – there was *absolutely* no dilemma. I knew I had to do it. I had known that since the moment Ratko was ordering the bombardment of Sarajevo. She couldn't be part of a caring profession without dissociating herself from that level of violence. Maybe what I'd underestimated was the father-daughter relationship. Maybe it was too deep to unpick. I can't fathom that. I have no experience of that. No matter. I had to face up to the moral imperative." He hoped those words – 'moral imperative' – didn't sound too pompous. He could think of no others that might capture his meaning.

Milan said nothing for a moment, then asked, "So, Goran, if I get what you're saying, you don't regret your ultimatum."

"You know, Milan, if you don't know me this sounds terrible but…" The tap to Goran's tears reopened. "I don't regret it. I *had* to do it…" He tried to compose himself; tried to ensure that their fellow drinkers in The Hole in the Wall didn't notice his distress. "But I never envisaged option three. Never imagined there was another option between choosing me or him. And I thought I'd reached a point where I held the stronger card." He paused.

Milan left some space unfilled again, then he exhaled vigorously. He needed some moments to come to terms with Goran's position statement. So he was taking part of the blame for Ana's death, but insisting that he had had no alternative to laying down the 'me or him' challenge. "Jeez, Goran – you don't half set yourself high hurdles to jump." He stopped to think, but he wanted to offer reassurance before Goran spoke again. "Look, you did what you thought was right. Okay? You thought you needed to make her face up to it: Hippocratic oath versus genocidal father. Maybe you're too pure, Goran. Maybe you should have left that as her dilemma to resolve. But you didn't. You forced the question. You didn't do it because you were a bad person. On the contrary, you did it because you wanted to put her in a clear moral space." Milan paused. "And it went terribly wrong... But it only went terribly wrong because you couldn't imagine yourself into her headspace. You couldn't measure the scale of her relationship with her father. No one could. But that's prompted action three. You couldn't have foreseen that. Hell, Goran, I know how much you loved her – but you can't hope to know what's going on in someone else's mind. Even someone you think you know intimately; even someone you think you can read intuitively."

There was a little more silence, then Milan said, "Goran, you're too hard on yourself. I love you and respect you for your integrity. Just don't – *don't* – beat yourself up when you made decisions for the right reasons… even if they had consequences you could never have imagined."

As he listened to Milan's words, Goran appreciated the warmth of his understanding, but he registered immediately the fact that his friends – Ana, Milan, Selveta – would tell him not to be so hard on himself; to cut himself the occasional bit of slack. But ultimately, he couldn't filter his conscience on a whim.

As they set off to walk home from the pub, Goran put his arm round Milan's shoulder for a moment. "Thanks, Milan. Thanks for listening."

"You're welcome, mate. But just stop beating yourself up. Really – you don't deserve it."

Both Goran and Milan were composed by the time they walked through the front door of Milan and Sandra's semi-detached home with its trim front lawn. Sandra would have detected none of the trauma of the past forty-five minutes. The smell of roast lamb curled through the hall invitingly.

Goran wasn't sure whether he would be able to stop beating himself up, but he was glad he had told Milan about his ultimatum to Ana. Milan's interpretation of the episode had been generous – but had it been accurate?

19

By the time Goran and Selveta landed in Sarajevo, this remarkable city was well on the way to patching itself back together again, albeit with the help of significant amounts of international aid.

Goran loved Belgrade but Sarajevo was something else. Belgrade was big and brash and unapologetically Serbian. Sarajevo by contrast encapsulated the whole story of Bosnia: often overrun but, even under occupation, tolerant, multi-ethnic, multi-faith, a jumble of architectural styles, an artistic and cultural melting pot. Goran would think he had captured its spirit, only to find, round another corner or in a tale he hadn't been told before, a whole new aspect.

He admitted privately to feeling some sense of guilt as a Serbian in a city Serbs and Bosnian Serbs had first tried to split and carve up and then pretty much tried to destroy. But Sarajevo had too much resilience and no one seemed to lay any blame at his door, even when they learned where he came from.

"You're helping our kids, brother. You're welcome here," was one comment. He liked being called 'brother' by a Sarajevan.

If the leaders behind the Dayton Agreement had been painfully slow to bring the wars to an end, even they recognised that it would be an abomination to split Bosnia's capital city into one Serbian quarter and another quarter into which every other ethnicity would be tipped. The blueprint that the Bosnian Serb leader Radovan Karadžić had claimed would put right an historic wrong was a non-starter. Sarajevo was quickly stitching back together its cosmopolitan fabric and remaking its cosmopolitan soul.

Yet Goran had limited space to enjoy the city to the full, so demanding was his new role. He couldn't imagine, when he was plying his mobile doctor trade in the hamlets and villages and depressed areas of Tuzla region, how demanding the administrative aspects of working in a big hospital in a capital city would be. He had to fight to ensure he ring-fenced sufficient time for clinical and pastoral work with his young patients. Of course, he had a team to manage and deploy and delegate to, and that required new skills far removed from those he had learned in medical school. But before long he had had a crashing realisation: no one teaches you those management skills; you just have to develop them as you go along with no manual in hand.

One aspect of his new role did fill him with enormous satisfaction. He had taken a gamble in insisting that he be accompanied in his new role by Selveta. As soon as he had landed, he had realised that there was an established and effective pastoral and social work team and structure in the hospital, and that, if he catapulted her to the top of that tree, it could provoke resentment and sour the atmosphere. He needn't have worried. Selveta exhibited all the delicacy and emotional intelligence that she had honed in Tuzla and gradually worked her way into the gaps in the structure, deftly picking up responsibilities that had been unmet, until the social work and managerial teams recognised her for the diamond that she was. She became a figure not just central to the unit, but cherished. His hunch that the move would be good for him and good for her had proved accurate – professionally, at least.

At weekends, when Selveta didn't go back to Tuzla to be with her family, she and Goran would play the tourist, getting to know each district of Sarajevo, picnicking among wild flowers on the foothills of Mount Trebević in the spring, crunching through the snow in winter, attending chamber or folk music events, or drinking Turkish coffee in their own Baščaršija area. An observer unacquainted with their story might have been intrigued by their relationship, wondering whether they were brother and sister, despite their very different appearances. And when she picked a flake of burek from his cheek over lunch in a local café, that observer would recognise an intimate action in a relationship that defied definition.

Which led Goran one day to ask himself explicitly where he was in his relationship with Ana. As time had passed, he had tried to ensure that her death didn't place her on a conveyor belt that would trundle her inevitably into the distance. Perhaps that explained why the photo of Ana remained on his sideboard despite Selveta's gentle suggestion. That dialogue that they had sustained so vividly in the aftermath of her demise had faded to an occasional crackle on the airwaves of his senses. Now and then, her voice would come at him as if loud and clear. More often he would be imagining how she might have reacted.

He couldn't talk to Selveta about it but he imagined that Milan might suggest to him that it was time to let Ana go; yet his position was unchanged from the time he had told Selveta that he couldn't rest until Ratko was arrested and taken off to The Hague. His and Ana's relationship would survive as a living, breathing organism at least until Ratko was captured, he acknowledged. *Oh, please, please, please, bring him to book soon*, he would plead to who knows which higher power.

But was he being unfair to Selveta? Was he booking her downtime as well as filling her working hours with endless tasks and challenges, and hence to some degree preventing her from settling down with someone else? She showed no signs of interest in any other man but she still appeared to be emotionally paralysed by the spectre of Ana in relation to him. In his frankest moments, Goran still didn't really know whether she held a candle for him that glowed brighter than the flame kindled by the proximity they dwelt in in their professional lives.

Goran was deeply disappointed that his professional duties prevented him from attending Milan and Sandra's wedding in Torquay. Try as he might, he just couldn't make it work. How long might it be before they had children? Not long, Goran suspected. And in different circumstances, where might he and Ana have been on that journey, he wondered? Another painful question too hard to try to answer.

And then he was snared. Photographs of a sickly, shrunken man were splashed over the front pages of Bosnia's newspapers. 'Butcher of Bosnia Seized' screamed one headline. As he took in the photographs of Ratko's capture and considered his now fragile frame, the word 'pathetic' formed in Goran's mind. He thought back to the portly man whose belly had tipped over his belt at the lunch table in Belgrade all those years ago. He thought back to the swagger and bravado. He thought back to the way that, in every room he entered, Ratko sucked the focus of attention his way, diminishing everyone else in his orbit. And Goran looked again at the photos. *Pathetic.* The word came back at him again, insistently. In some of the photos Goran felt he read in Ratko's eyes a reaction that Ana's father may never have experienced before: fear. The man who had tried to break Sarajevo, who had heartlessly sent thousands of Srebrenican menfolk to their deaths, now in his later years was learning what it was like to feel hunted.

"Bastard!" Goran whispered venomously. But the word felt inadequate.

Before long Selveta was knocking at his door. "I thought I'd better come round. Make sure you're okay," she said.

"Thanks, Selveta."

She looked a little uncomfortable, as if unsure as to whether she might be the unwelcome guest at a wake. Might these moments be Ana moments that she should absent herself from? "Let me know if you want to be alone," she said. "But I had to check to make sure you were okay."

Typically selfless, thought Goran. She didn't know whether he wanted her to share these moments with him, but his well-being made her face up to her discomfort. "Yes, I think I'm okay. It's what I wanted more than anything, wasn't it? It's just I'm feeling a bit numb at the moment. Not sure how to react, you know," he said.

"Do you want me to leave you alone for a bit? Or do you want company?"

Goran wanted her to go. At this moment he wanted a separation between these two chapters in his life. "No, no – please stay," he said. "I'll make coffee."

"No. Let me." And Selveta took off her coat and drifted quietly into the neutral space of the kitchen.

The phone rang. It was Danijel. Goran was touched by how assiduous Milan's father was with his updates. Always with the inside track, always alert to the fact that Goran was near the front of a line of those deserving to be informed early of the true details of the story.

"It took a little longer than I'd expected," said Danijel, "but as I forecast, the calibre of the people prepared to protect him just kept diminishing."

Mladić had been housed in military VIP locations at first, living the life of Riley, but after Milošević was lifted, year by year his guardians had peeled away.

"They found him in a scruffy room with just a little electric heater on the first floor of his cousin Branislav's dilapidated farmhouse in Lazarevo," said Danijel. Lazarevo was an unremarkable village ninety kilometres north of Belgrade, home to two sets of Ratko's cousins. "It transpired he'd been holed up there for at least three years, receiving no visitors. He was afraid his closest family would be tracked, so – apart from his cousin – it was pretty much total solitude."

Goran found it hard to imagine how a man with a short span of attention and a love of the centre stage could have coped with that.

"He'd had a stroke during that time but he wouldn't allow the family to take him for or to seek treatment. He was more frightened of capture than of a sad, lonely death," said Danijel.

He told Goran that Ratko had looked so frail, so unlike the strutting, forceful Mladić who had featured so prominently on TV screens during the wars, that the officers from the special war crimes unit couldn't believe it was him.

"They asked him who he was, and apparently he said, 'You've found who you're looking for. I'm Ratko Mladić.'

"The thing is, Goran, he had sworn he'd never be taken alive. He had told his cousin that he had to shoot him rather than give him up. But Branislav would never have shot him. And he had his own Heckler & Koch handgun under a pile of dirty washing in the room he was arrested in. When push came to shove, he either lacked the courage to take his own life – or decided not to."

"Unlike my Ana," said Goran.

"Indeed," said Danijel.

There was a natural pause to their exchanges as the depth of that piece of irony sunk into Goran.

"There's one more detail you need to know, Goran. Before they flew him out to The Hague, they did grant him one last request. He asked to visit his daughter's grave, and they took him to Topčider. Gave him forty-five minutes on his own. They say that his minders could see his lips move… as if he was chatting to her."

The detail seared into Goran's soul. What if he had been there, sitting on the bench by the grave, when Ratko had landed? How horrific might that have been? As he let the thought sink in, he begrudgingly acknowledged that it was an act of compassion from Ratko's captors that reflected well on them, but part of him felt outraged, as if his – Goran's – sacred space had been invaded by a monster. *We both loved her and we both lost her*, Goran reflected silently. And he shrugged, but he was hurting badly inside. Personal pain and fury at Ratko ebbed and flowed.

Selveta had emerged with coffee halfway through the call with Danijel. She was clearly aware of the nature of the phone conversation. She looked even more uncomfortable than she had appeared when she had first arrived at Goran's flat. She raised her eyebrows as he came off the call, the gesture indicating that she was available to hear any insights without her taking the liberty of asking a question outright that might be maladroit. Goran felt a pang of gratitude towards her. His thoughts were whirling, but despite that, he recognised the efforts she was making and the discomfort she was going through just to offer him her support in these appalling moments.

"He didn't have the courage to do away with himself, Selveta. Ana did. He didn't." Goran uttered the words looking into the distance rather than directly at her.

"Well, I'm not sure we want more deaths, do we?" She paused. "Perhaps it's better if he's brought to justice." She looked away. Goran sensed she wasn't sure whether her commentary was appropriate at this stage.

"Maybe you're right," he said.

She turned and made her way back into the kitchen, emerging a minute later with a generous shot of brandy in a tumbler. "Here, Goran. Drink this. It'll do you good."

He took the glass and tried to crack a smile. Though many of her family did, she didn't drink. He appreciated the gesture. The alcohol hit the back of his throat with considerable force. *That's why they call it a shot*, he thought.

But after he had settled for a few moments, Goran felt hollow. He had expected to feel relief upon Ratko's incarceration – perhaps even joy. But it was nothing like that. He sipped at his drink again and reflected that he needed to give himself time to let all the pieces land where they fell and see what he could make of them after a period of reflection.

Selveta approached him and laid her hand on his arm. "Goran, just say if you want me to stay with you tonight… if you need company."

Goran wasn't shocked by the offer, though he hadn't foreseen it. From her demeanour, he knew she was thinking solely of his welfare. He put a hand on her shoulder. "Selveta, that's very kind of you… but not tonight."

"And will you be okay?" she asked.

"Yes, I'll be okay, I think… No, I'm sure." And he tried to smile again but he couldn't summon up the conviction.

A few days later, Goran managed to get through to Milan. Like Goran, in the days since his arrest was announced Milan had landed on the detail that Ratko had vowed to kill himself rather than be caught, and then had not followed through. Both Goran and Milan had concluded that he had lacked the courage to do so. Neither of them was of any other view than that he had shown enormous amounts of bravery at many moments in his military career – even if it was bravery in pursuit of misguided goals.

"But you know what, Milan? At the end of the day, he bottled it. Pathetic, eh?" That word emerged again from within Goran.

"I tend to agree," said Milan.

"My friend, Selveta – she said we don't need or want any more deaths, and I think that's right. She says it's better justice runs its course." Goran paused and, though Milan obviously couldn't see from the other end of the line in Torquay, he looked down at his feet, then added, with a degree of bitterness in his tone, "Milan, I think of Ana in her flat that night with the gun. And I think of how scared she must have been. I can hardly bear to think about how scared she must have been – and yet she went ahead and pulled the trigger. Did the deed." He paused again. "You know, I wish I could have it out with him, Milan. Say to Ratko, 'She pulled the trigger, so why did you choose to hang around on this stinking planet?' I'd like to know what he'd say."

It was hard for Milan to know how to respond to the depth of Goran's emotions, so he just muttered, "Yeah, yeah. It's terrible, isn't it?"

"Anyway – enough of that," said Goran, trying to pull himself together again. "How's married life?"

"Couldn't be better, Goran. Couldn't be better. And what about you? How's it going in Sarajevo?"

"It's tough work but it's satisfying. And I love the city… but I might just take a bit of a break. You know, to get over this stuff. I think I need to go back to Belgrade for a few days. Try to get this out of my system."

"Well, look after yourself, Goran. Remember – you're always welcome here. And remember – this is what we wanted. The old bugger banged up. Maybe you – *we* – can move on from here."

Goran hung up. He had been glad to share withering judgements of Ratko with someone else who really knew him but, the call finished, he sat down in his armchair, made a church ceiling shape with the tips of his fingers, and let his mind drift free. After a while, he said out loud, "Ana, are you there?" Not a sound or even a crackle on his network. And then he thought of sweet, kind Selveta. Yet he realised he felt utterly alone.

20

There was a knock at Goran's door. He felt mildly irritated as he had been writing a letter to Milan and had been in full flow. It was almost complete. He put down his fountain pen and went to the door. It was Selveta.

"Oh, hi," said Goran. He felt slightly ashamed because he knew he had been more remote with her in the few days since Ratko's arrest – but his excuse to himself was that he had been more remote with everyone. He had slipped deeper into himself, and a kind of melancholy just short of self-pity had settled upon him. It was just that, subconsciously, he had asked more of Selveta than of his other work colleagues, and he knew that she had given him more as well. They had never articulated it but her support to him went beyond the professional. She didn't deserve to be pushed to arm's length along with everyone else. Her appearance at his door was her affirmation that she had some rights in this relationship, however unspoken. "Come in, come in," he said. As she stepped in, he took a couple of paces towards his writing desk and tucked the letter to Milan under a sheet of blotting paper. He thought she may have spotted his move – but no matter.

"Er... Goran." Selveta was nervous, clearly unsure whether she had the right to quiz him. "I know you're probably still in shock about Ratko, but the guys in the unit told me you were going away. To Belgrade. For a few days." She was flustered but she pressed on. "I thought you might have told me, but more important – you know we've got that unit strategy day on Friday. You can't miss that."

Goran tried to look inscrutable. "I just thought it might be an idea if the rest of you had a go at framing the strategy... without me. Might make for some fresh ideas…" As he heard himself utter the words, he knew they sounded ridiculous. He tried to assume a look of conviction.

"Oh, Goran – come off it! That's nonsense." Selveta turned away from him. "Anyway, I've cancelled it. Said we'll hold it when you get back."

She traced out a little circle across the carpet. Goran realised he hadn't yet asked her to take off her coat.

"Oh… okay. That's fine. I just thought… That's all." He knew Selveta had seen straight through his attempt at 'conviction'. "But do take off your coat, Selveta."

"Thank you." She hung it on the back of a chair. "Look, Goran. It's understandable that you're in a bit of turmoil. But don't retreat into yourself. This is the time when you need your friends and colleagues."

Inside his head, Goran was saying to himself, *I absolutely need to retreat into myself now. No one else can help me or tell me what to do… usefully.* But of course, he didn't say that out loud.

"By all means take some time in Belgrade, if you think that'll help clear your head. But I promise you: internalising everything isn't the way to resolve this." She looked at him with a certain sternness. "Believe me, Goran. I know a bit about this stuff."

It was the closest she had come to pulling rank on him. And he recalled the way in which she had managed the traumas of Elvedin in the hamlet of Čaklovići Gornji. He felt chastened. Of course she knew more about 'this stuff' than he did.

"I'm sorry, Selveta. I should have told you…" He ruffled his hair with his fingers.

"So when are you off?" she asked.

"First thing tomorrow."

"And how long are you away?"

"At least three days – maybe five. Depends."

"Okay…" Selveta looked down at the carpet. Goran knew she was irritated.

"Look – I was just about to do some food," he said. "Will you have some pasta with me?"

Selveta smiled weakly. "Yes, that would be nice. Thank you."

Goran slipped off into the kitchen. Selveta didn't at first follow him.

Goran sensed that there was an element of her making him pay for his remoteness by a little remoteness of her own.

When she did wander through into the kitchen several minutes later, she had a question for him that no one else would have framed, let alone asked. "Goran – sorry, I'm being nosy again, but you've got your bags packed. Are you really taking your doctor's bag to Belgrade? You're not planning any freelancing in Belgrade, are you? You haven't got an interview back there, have you?" And she laughed, as if to suggest that her question was preposterous, not serious.

"No – no. I just love that bag…" Goran was looking at the boiling pan of pasta, so he could conceal the fact that even he knew that that comment was lame.

They ate dinner together. Goran relaxed a little, but he acknowledged that Selveta would have registered their conversation as being atypical Goran. He felt some shame – but he didn't feel he could do any more at that moment.

As Selveta went to leave, he couldn't think of a plausible reason for it but he said to her, "Selveta, will you take a key for the flat? Just in case…"

Selveta clearly didn't know what 'just in case' meant but, perhaps because his general behaviour that evening had bordered on strange, she said simply, "Yes, of course", and pocketed the key.

On the threshold, he hugged her a little more tightly than he normally would. He hoped that, alongside his handing her a key to his flat, it wouldn't send out alarm signals.

The following morning he had to queue at the post office to have his letter to the UK stamped and dispatched as an express delivery before he took the coach to Belgrade. He was told that the letter would be with Milan in three days.

He had expected that the nine-hour coach trip to Belgrade would give him plenty of time to think, to try to reconcile things – but while his thoughts swirled, they led him nowhere new. Occasionally he felt a pang of shame at the way he had treated Selveta recently, but as each pang kicked in, he tried to suppress it. He wasn't proud of himself for that.

When he awoke in the flat that he had kept on as his Belgrade base, he reflected that he would have one full day ahead of him before Milan received his letter. There might then be 'consequences', but of course, he had no idea what they might be or whether or how they might affect him. Those consequences might be too late anyway. One consequence would certainly be Milan calling his Sarajevo number. He imagined the sound of the phone ringing harshly in the empty flat with no one to field it.

Of course, his principal duty ahead of his own version of D-day was to make the pilgrimage to Ana's grave. He was fortunate. The weather was beautiful with only a dappling of cloud brushed across the back of a clean blue sky. He felt some trepidation as he approached, then relief as he realised no one was in the vicinity. He sat down on the bench and, instinctively, he made the sign of the cross. He was momentarily shocked by the automaticity of the gesture. Perhaps the time he had spent in the presence of so many World Vision staff while in Tuzla had normalised the action for him. Perhaps he had subconsciously absorbed the soothing effect making the sign appeared to have on his colleagues. Perhaps that had prompted it.

He tried to open his soul to Ana at that moment, but it felt as though there was an obstacle between them. Then he imagined the scene a few days earlier when the security team had escorted Ratko to the cemetery, led him up to Ana's grave and then stepped back – a ring of steel around him still, but at a distance. Would he have sat down in contemplation? Sat down on this very bench? Or, with his short span of attention, would he have walked round with a kind of suppressed frenzy bubbling away inside him? Goran imagined Ratko issuing expressions of love for Ana to the open air, intermingled with mutterings; with near-deranged assertions of self-justification and guiltlessness.

But something physical had changed in the environment; something that in Goran's eyes added lustre to the scenery. Though it was two kilometres distant, the magnificent Ada Bridge, leading traffic westwards out of Belgrade over the Sara River, now filled a gap in the trees at the opposite end of the cemetery to where Ana's grave lay. Its single pillar with cables on either side like the strings of a harp splaying from it reminded Goran of the long-necked lute, the saz, that he had heard Selveta's father play so skilfully and so movingly on the music night she had arranged some years back in Tuzla. The juxtaposition of Ana's understated headstone and this symbol of his journey away from her, west to Tuzla and to Bosnia, seemed appropriate in that moment – perhaps even comforting.

He didn't try to wring too much emotion from his time at Ana's graveside. He felt he risked trying to force it and he wasn't able to generate a special feeling. Loss, yes. Grief, yes – but a superior kind of exaltation eluded him in those moments.

As he walked away, less than a hundred metres from Ana's grave, half a dozen nuns were swabbing and polishing clean the headstone and slab of a large tomb containing the remains of multiple Little Sisters of Jesus who had passed away in their Belgrade convent over the past forty years. In their sky-blue tunics and white veils, they went about their task assiduously. Goran felt that they glowed with satisfaction at a job performed thoroughly and with love. He was minded to speak to them; to tell them about his loss. Their empathy would have been a given and they would have blessed him and promised prayers for Ana. But he didn't. He felt a slight twinge of regret as he exited the east gate to the cemetery and then headed back down the hill to the city.

On his D-day, Goran visited his parents. It was comforting to be back in the family home but he knew that his mother and father had found him quiet, and although they touched upon the arrest of Ratko, he knew they knew why he was quiet.

The day after his D-day, the phone rang in the flat a few times and he knew it was Selveta. He didn't pick up. That evening he took a walk to the Skadarlija district in the east of the city. For good reasons he hadn't walked through its cobbled streets or experienced its bohemian atmosphere since Ana had gone. It was the route he took to his and Ana's favourite café, the Aviator. It would be his first return to the establishment since she had died. It had been a watering hole they had stumbled upon after a walk through Skadarlija. They had found it cool and understated, attracting a young, creative clientele. They had always liked to sit at one of the tables at the back where there was a turquoise velvet banquette with black button studs. Although it was years since he'd been there and for some time he had not wanted to return without her, he now felt ready to go back there. He felt that it might bring back memories of happy times rather than prompt nightmares.

In his favourite seat on the banquette, a man Goran estimated to be in his late thirties was sitting. He was reading a copy of *The Times* of London and Goran could tell from the front-page headlines that it was today's edition. He was clearly English, though when he ordered his coffee he spoke fluent Serbo-Croat with perhaps a slight hint of a Croatian dialect. Goran concluded he had flown out most likely from London to Belgrade that day, bringing his newspaper with him.

Goran was intrigued, and in normal circumstances he felt he would have tried to strike up a conversation with him and find out his business. But the heavy hand on his heart and the incessant debate going on in his head about what to do next left him feeling too vulnerable for a conversation the direction of which he could not forecast.

The Englishman folded up his copy of *The Times* and stepped out into the evening air. Now Goran would never know who he was. He felt a mild regret at not having satisfied his curiosity.

When he awoke the following morning, aware that it had been two days since Milan had received his letter, he knew it had to be what they called in sport 'moving day': the day when the outcome of a tournament begins to take shape. He had to act on this day or risk the initiative passing to third parties, disabling his power to shape his own destiny.

But first things first. He had to visit Ana's grave again. Then he would be in a position to make a decision.

He never minded the length of the walk up to the cemetery: through the well-heeled parts of Senjak, then along the road that weaved by thin woods till you crossed the bridge over the trickle of a river and, round the corner, the headstones hove into view.

As he approached Ana's section of the cemetery, he started. There was someone sitting on the bench by her grave. It wasn't her brother, Darko, and obviously it wasn't Ratko. Goran took a detour, circling round to get closer while appearing not to be approaching. And then, from a clear viewpoint, a shock thumped into his core. The man sitting on the bench by his Ana was the man he had seen in the Aviator café the night before. He was jotting notes into a small black pocketbook, then taking in the panorama. Was he looking down at the Ada Bridge? Did he realise how new an addition to the skyline it was? But above all, why had he chosen to sit by Ana's grave? Goran had to know – yet he couldn't know.

The more he thought about it, given the recent arrest of Ratko, the more he came to the conclusion that this was an English journalist – but one who knew not just Ana's father's story, but her story too. If Goran was right, he couldn't introduce himself and probe the man, because he would be probed back. He, who had side-swerved the pack of journalists pursuing his scent in the days after Ana's death, could not afford to be tracked down now.

The development caused Goran to tremble for a while, so shocked was he by this coincidence. The journalist, as Goran now deemed him, spent a good thirty minutes by Ana's grave, looking around the cemetery and taking notes of features of the surroundings. And if Goran wanted his own time by the graveside, when the man went to leave Topčider, Goran felt he had to follow him at a distance – undetected if possible, of course.

Goran was intrigued at first when the man he was sleuthing turned right at the east gate of the cemetery and heading south instead of taking the route north that would lead him back towards the city centre. But, once he began following the winding roads through light woodland, parkland, and affluent developments, Goran became increasingly convinced that he knew where the journalist was heading. When he wiggled through some backstreets and turned left, Goran knew he was right, but he was no less shocked to be proved right.

Goran had to cross the road and stay at a distance but, sure enough, the man stopped at Blagoja Parovića 119 – the once-handsome house where the Mladićs had lived, where he had Sunday-lunched with Ana and her family, and on the lawn of which property he had first met his now good friend Milan. The house looked scruffy and unoccupied – far removed from the affluent, comfortable home it had been some twenty years earlier. The journalist stopped in front of it. He scribbled in bursts in his pocketbook, then turned and looked to the panorama south where, just a few kilometres away, Belgrade proper ended and open fields rolled.

There was now no doubt. This *was* a British journalist. Might he be a staff member of *The Times*? And what was certain was that there would shortly be a piece in that or a similar British newspaper about Ratko and Ana. Though Goran's curiosity was consuming him, his situation paralysed him. He couldn't approach the journalist, or he would become part of that story. Perhaps even a major part of the story, if the journalist were canny enough and Goran were to be sweet-talked into spilling the beans that he had – beans that would represent rich fare for a journalist who spoke Serbo-Croat fluently and who clearly had a specialist knowledge of the fall of Yugoslavia.

For a few moments Goran was tempted. Why not approach him? Why not tell him what had happened? It might be a relief. Ratko was banged up now. He was no threat. Yes – but he still had family and friends. They were mainly bad people who would seek horrible retribution if even a scintilla of his story were to be published. Goran turned on his heel and fled – insofar as anyone could flee at a pace that would not attract attention.

The encounter threw a bunch of new, hard questions at Goran as he picked his way back north with an urgency he didn't quite understand. He went back to the cemetery and had his time with Ana, though the peaceful session he had envisaged had been rendered impossible by the emergence of Mr *Times* of London. Another sign of the cross by the grave. What was that about? Where had that come from? And then he walked and trotted back to town. If he had hoped to wind down on 'moving day' as calmly as he could, he had been thwarted. His mind raced, new questions hurling themselves into his head until he could barely take any more.

Back in his flat, he sat in his favourite armchair. He had imagined making his decision tranquilly. Instead he was on high alert. A piece of what he had thought was his own unique, private, personal situation was about to be blazed across a British newspaper with international reach. He went into the kitchen and poured himself a brandy that was three fingers deep – three times his usual measure.

Should he? Could he? He let the questions roll around his mind for some minutes. He hadn't decided yet whether he should or shouldn't, whether he could or couldn't. He took a slug of brandy, fetched the black leather doctor's bag on which Selveta had remarked, and sat down, the bag between his feet. He unclipped it. There were six boxes arranged neatly in there. He hadn't decided whether he should or could, whether he shouldn't or couldn't, but he would take a look at the tools that might decide his destiny. He pulled out the top white cardboard box. Instead of there being foil-packed sheets of sedatives, there was nothing. He gasped. He flipped through each of the first five boxes. Empty. Then he opened the sixth with a sense of what was either foreboding or expectation.

There was a sheet of writing paper folded in quarters that he recognised as one peeled from the block he had used to write to Milan. His name, written in the black ink of his fountain pen in Selveta's handwriting, was on the top. He unfolded it precisely, daunted but a little excited to read what was in it.

Dear Goran, it read.

I read the letter to Milan that you were finishing when I arrived at your flat. You're not absolutely explicit but I fear I understand what you were thinking. That's why you'll find I've removed the sedatives and flushed them away.

As soon as – underlined *– you read this note, pick up the phone and call me before you do anything else. For the years that I have put my emotional life on hold, you owe me this.*

And by the way, if you doubted this or didn't notice it, I love you.

Your Selveta xxx

So many points swirled around, and he would have to go back forensically and address each one. But the detail that landed with him – perhaps because it was the last in her letter – was that she had signed it 'Your Selveta', not 'Yours, Selveta'.

Without reflecting upon it for a moment, he picked up the phone and he dialled her number.

21

Goran could remember passages of his letter to Milan pretty much by heart. It had been such an important letter, and its contents so considered, that he was hardly surprised that its key sections were etched on his memory.

When we were last together in England, we talked about how I had given Ana an ultimatum the day before she died: she had to choose between her father and me. If she wouldn't renounce him, I would walk away from her. And you suggested it must have been some dilemma: issuing the ultimatum or letting things slide. And you'll remember that I insisted that there was no dilemma. I had to do it, and though I mourn and will mourn till the day I die the choice she made, I still believe that.

Goran reflected that because, unbeknown to him, she had read his letter to Milan even before he had sent it, Selveta was now only the second person in the world to learn that his ultimatum was a factor in Ana's death. Or perhaps the third, if Milan had shared his secret with Sandra.

There was, however, one real dilemma that I did face, and it was one in which you were unwittingly involved. That time you and Ratko made a flying visit to Belgrade and you popped in to see me? You'll remember that you had to nip out to the pharmacy to pick up some medication for Ratko because he was concerned that he was running low. And then you shot up to town to pick up some new books, as you were low on reading material. Irrelevant detail, but I recall your being particularly thrilled at picking up the latest Philip Roth novel.

I'm slightly ashamed to say it, Milan, but while you were out at the bookshop, I fished Ratko's drugs out of your holdall. I wanted to see the condition he was being treated for. It was pretty clear that they were for a heart condition and, if he were to go for any time without that medication, he would almost certainly die. The body becomes reliant on the drugs once that kind of treatment is introduced. That is highly likely to have been what happened to Milošević when he died. He simply stopped taking his drugs.

It struck me at that moment that I had bottles of placebos in my flat that we medical students use when we are carrying out experiments on groups of volunteers who are helping us assess the efficacy of new treatments. Milan, I went so far as to count out two months' worth of placebos, and I havered over whether I should swap Ratko's heart pills for my placebos. I was literally holding them in the palm of my hand as I weighed up the choice I had to make. He would think he was continuing to take his medication, but there would have been a very high chance that he would die because he wasn't. No one would have realised what had happened. It could have been, if you like, the perfect crime.

In the event, I popped the sixty or so pills I'd counted out back into their bottle and I didn't swap them for his drugs. Just as my thinking was that Ana could not morally swear her Hippocratic oath without renouncing her father, so I struggled with reconciling the oath I would swear with an action that would be highly likely to lead to the premature death of one of 'my patients'.

But that's not the end of it. Think on this. At around that time, you were forecasting to me that things weren't looking good in those towns and villages on Bosnia's eastern border with Serbia. You mentioned to me your particular fears for the people of Srebrenica.

Thinking of the situation now, I honestly believe that, if I had swapped Ratko's drugs for placebos, he would likely have died, and I do not believe that, without his leadership, without his orders, a pogrom on the scale of the Srebrenica tragedy would have occurred. Let's say around seven thousand people died or went missing, never *to be seen again. I don't doubt that some people would have died but I HONESTLY BELIEVE I COULD HAVE SPARED AT LEAST FIVE THOUSAND PEOPLE FROM SLAUGHTER, HAD I MADE A DIFFERENT DECISION AND REMOVED HIM FROM THE SCENE. It hardly bears thinking about, does it?*

Do I feel guilty about it? I'm not sure. Do I have regrets about it? Yes, I certainly have. Would I have behaved differently had I known how many lives I could have saved? It sounds like a no-brainer but I'd have been invalidating any future Hippocratic oath I'd swear; I'd have committed a crime. Yet – one life versus five thousand! Might I not have been able to make the case from the dock? Morally, yes. Legally, probably not. Not that at the time I thought this all through rationally and logically. I didn't. I held the placebos in my hand – and then I put them away.

So, Milan – there was no dilemma about confronting Ana, though huge sorrow at the fact that she conjured up a 'get-out' I could never have envisaged. There was a huge dilemma when I held those placebos in the palm of my hand and knew I could bring about Ratko's early demise. Probably only Hippocrates, a fourth- and fifth-century BC Greek physician, hauled me back from that.

So, Milan, I am trying to write this as calmly as I can, but can you imagine how tough it has been to deal with the knowledge that I was partly to blame for Ana's death, but I was also partly 'to blame' for the death of around five thousand Srebrenicans? I'm not looking for sympathy; I just wanted you, as probably my best extant friend, to know that, if you ever found me frenetic or too preoccupied by the Mladić question, then these are the reasons why.

Goran remembered too the way in which he had signed off his letter.

Milan, I want to sign off by letting you know what a good friend you have been to me. Though we only corresponded and spoke occasionally, I always felt we were kindred spirits and that I could bounce off you my frustrations – in relation to Ratko in particular. I always felt you acted with the best motives. I hope you felt that I tried to do so too.

I'm not sure where I'm going, but whatever happens, I wish you and Sandra a happy and fulfilling life, blessed with children, if that is what you both want. I see you both sharing a relationship that will grow ever stronger. I may not see you again. I want to see whether I can find my way back to my Ana – but, as I said when you left my flat having quit Ratko and the army, I wish you godspeed.

With gratitude for your friendship, and with all my love, now and forever.

Goran

Goran and Selveta had stepped off a plane at London Heathrow and were making their way through the airport, having cleared passport control and customs. Goran glanced at the newspaper rack at the front of WH Smith. He made a double-take, then swooped over and picked up The Times.

It wasn't the lead item, but a front-page story running down the strap was headlined 'Missing: "saintly" Serbian medic who blamed himself for five thousand Srebrenica deaths'. The byline read 'By Mick Morrison, Belgrade'. So the man Goran had seen in the Aviator café, by Ana's grave and in front of the Mladić household had been Milan's journalist friend; the journalist who had clinched the 'just one match' scoop when Ratko had threatened to bomb Washington or London if his men were bombed by NATO planes.

Mick's story recounted the details of Goran's letter to Milan: Goran's ultimatum to Ana, his placebo dilemma, and his fear that he was partly responsible for thousands of deaths in Srebrenica. While it was shocking to see his darkest secrets in print, shared with thousands of readers, Goran appreciated that Milan would have contacted Mick Morrison and explained the background to his disappearance purely out of concern for him. He was missing, perhaps disturbed by the long-awaited arrest of his girlfriend's father.

A spokesman for his Sarajevo hospital told The Times *that Dr Goran Nikolić had taken leave and was believed to be in Belgrade and they had no reason to be concerned about his well-being.*

But a Serbian close friend, Milan Tešević, now a schoolteacher in Torquay, said he had received a letter in which the doctor implied that he may take his own life.

"Goran is a wonderful doctor and a man I'd describe as almost saintly in his concern for others. But sometimes he sets himself impossibly high moral standards. He had been worried for many years that Ratko Mladić might escape justice. He always said his 'task' would be complete once Ratko was arrested and taken to The Hague.

"He recently revealed to me that he had issued an ultimatum to his girlfriend, Ratko's daughter, challenging her to renounce her father because of his atrocities in the wars. He believed the ultimatum might have hastened her death, and I think he blames himself partly for her suicide. I just hope that he has not done anything rash, and that he is able to live to see General Mladić convicted and incarcerated for a very long time, if not for life," said Mr Tešević.

The front-page story ran onto an inside page and, alongside it on page four, Mick Morrison had written a more personal commentary, featuring details observed during his visit to Topčider Cemetery that Goran had witnessed. It was illustrated with an agency photograph of Ana's grave.

The headstone is all but unmarked. All around it are graves that tell multiple stories. Politicians, scientists and military leaders jostle silently for the passer-by's attention, their headshots and the snatched summaries of their lives reaching out. Yet this simple charcoal-grey headstone and slab conceal perhaps the most poignant story to have graced the vast Topčider Cemetery in over a century of its history.

The headstone reads simply, 'Mladic, Ana – 1971–1994'. It reveals no family details or connections. It offers no explanation for the death of a woman at the age of just twenty-three.

Ana Mladić was in fact the daughter of Bosnian Serb General Ratko Mladić, who was arrested and taken to The Hague Tribunal two weeks ago. After his case is heard, he is likely to be incarcerated for life for his part in atrocities including the deaths of around seven thousand people from Srebrenica in Bosnia in 1995. Ana had been a medical student in Belgrade, and this week a detail emerged that added further poignancy to her tragic story.

Ana was believed to have committed suicide out of shame at the atrocities carried out by her father. Yet The Times has learned that her demise may have been hastened by her boyfriend, Dr Goran Nikolić, who had also been a student at the medical faculty in Belgrade. He has revealed to friends that back in 1994, one year before the Srebrenica massacres, he had issued her with an ultimatum: she had to renounce her father or he would leave her. He could never have imagined that, rather than choose one or the other, she would choose a third option that he had never foreseen: she committed suicide, using one of her father's ceremonial pistols.

The pain suffered by Ana as she faced up to her destiny is described nowhere. Her grave reveals none of the trauma. Yet we must hope and pray that one of the saddest stories Topčider conceals is not added to by another death: that of Dr Nikolić, the boyfriend who unwittingly issued her with an impossible challenge.

Goran had bought the paper and sat down on an airport bench to read both stories before passing it to Selveta to read.

As she completed the second story, she squeezed Goran's arm and said quietly, "Like I said. No more deaths."

Goran reflected that on the day that he had seen Mick Morrison in the Aviator café, Mick would have been informed of the contents of his letter to Milan earlier in the day, then jumped on a plane to Belgrade to scout Ana's grave.

Goran and Selveta got up and headed off towards the Underground, which would take them to Paddington, from where they would take the train to Torquay.

Three nights earlier, Selveta had answered the phone in her Sarajevo flat.

"Selveta here."

"Selveta… It's Goran."

There was a silence.

"I'm *so* sorry," he said. Goran wasn't sure for which aspect of his behaviour he was offering an apology, but the moment seemed to call for one. And his apology was sincere.

"Goran, I'm so glad you called." There was a further silence as each tried to work their way through the awkwardness of the moment, and then Selveta spoke again. "Come home, Goran," she said softly. She paused, then said, "Just come home."

Goran was completely floored. At a stroke, with just two words – come home – she had reoriented him both geographically and emotionally. It was miraculous. For a few seconds he was speechless as the implications seeped in. She was saying to him that his home was now in Bosnia. He – the city boy from Belgrade, Serbia! She was saying too that his emotional home was with her, Selveta. And she was saying it delicately but sufficiently firmly for it to be clear that she wasn't expecting any pushback. And he realised that her insights and her subtlety and precision in expressing those insights gave her enormous power – though he knew that it was a power she would only ever exercise responsibly and for the benefit of those touched by her.

The silence was expanding and Goran realised he had to fill it. "I will, Selveta. I will."

In hindsight Goran wondered just how much Selveta had planned ahead and how much she had ad-libbed in the moment, but she was quickly into practicalities.

"Take the first coach tomorrow morning to Sarajevo. I'll find out when it's due and I'll be waiting for you at the bus station."

After their brief call had ended, Goran looked at the huge measure of brandy he had poured himself. He meticulously trickled two thirds of it back into the bottle without spilling any, he sipped at what was left and enjoyed that initial tang, then he sat back to try to make sense of what had happened in the last hour.

His overwhelming sensation was one of relief. Not relief at the fact that he had contemplated overdosing and had stepped back from that. No – it was a relief born of Selveta's reorientation of his life. So unexpected, so instantaneous, so radical. And he realised that what she had done with those two words – come home – was to adjust the balance of their relationship: subtly, but with enormous implications. Out of the blue he had gone from fighting internally every battle, every moral question, utterly alone. Now, without even having stepped down from the coach in Sarajevo and hugged her, he realised he had a support mechanism. He wouldn't need to toil and worry alone. He might not even have to worry at all.

When he thought through how he had arrived at this destination, he realised that in his professional relationships, including with Selveta, it was always the qualified doctor that was viewed as the senior partner. All other players deferred to him. But, in that brief phone exchange between Belgrade and Sarajevo, she had gently shifted the balance of the relationship. She had assumed a role in which she was no longer the junior in the relationship. But rather than feel a loss of control – men tended to like control; they expected control, he thought – Goran felt a sweet relief course through him. The challenges he had been facing alone they would face together, but now guided more firmly by her instincts. And of course, her instincts were superior to his own.

As he stepped down from the coach the following afternoon and they hugged and the driver unlocked the luggage panel along the side of the bus and began dumping cases on the pavement, Goran was aware that they needed to slip into this next phase of their relationship gradually. He sensed that Selveta appreciated this too. They wouldn't charge at it, but their trajectory was now set.

In the early evening, in Goran's flat after he had unpacked, Selveta sat opposite him and her face took on a sternness that he had seen before. Goran knew he was in for a gentle telling-off for the way he had behaved since Ratko had been grabbed. And maybe some time before that too.

"Goran," she said, "you were wrong to put Milan in that position, you know. I know he's your go-to man on things Ratko, but really – he called up the unit and they tracked me down and I had to try to reassure him that you wouldn't have done anything daft."

"And did you know that I wouldn't do anything daft?"

"Yeah – I was pretty sure. I wouldn't have let you go to Belgrade if I hadn't been confident. And after I'd read the letter and confiscated your sedatives and scribbled you that note… Well, I didn't think you would feel able to ignore it. That's why I told the hospital to put out a statement suggesting we weren't concerned.

"But by then you'd put the wind up Milan, and he'd already contacted his friend Mick on *The Times*. He was in quite a state." Selveta paused and looked down. "So what we're going to do is fly to England the day after tomorrow. I've told Milan and Sandra that we'll go and stay with them in Torquay for a few days. We owe them an apology. *You* owe them an apology." She gave a little smile at her own audacity. "But anyway, you could do with a complete change of scenery and plenty of company. *We* could do with a complete change of scenery and plenty of company." And she smiled again, this time more widely.

But then the sternness returned, and Goran knew he had more penance to pay.

"There's another thing you need to know, though, Goran. I've seen it a lot in you medical types," she began.

Goran smiled inwardly at being labelled 'a medical type'.

"You spend your days healing others and it's tough, but you feel good about it. So much so that, at the end of the working day, subconsciously you think you've done enough. You switch off that tap of empathy and compassion. You put your nurturing into neutral. I've seen it so many times with GPs. It's why so many of them have broken marriages. And in your case the effect was exacerbated by everything you went through with Ana – both before and after her death. I know you, Goran, and you're a good man, but over the years, your insistence on doing the right thing, the pure thing – well, it turned you in on yourself. You were probably too hard on Ana. How she dealt with her father should have been her choice. Not yours."

The briskness of this analysis of the pivotal moment in his life initially took his breath away. He said nothing. Then he admired its bravery. He wasn't sure whether or not he agreed with it.

"And then you spent the years after her death beating yourself up. And then Srebrenica! Goran, it *wasn't* your doing. It *wasn't* your fault." She had raised her voice at this point – in frustration rather than anger. "But you know – and I admit I'm being super harsh here – it became a little self-indulgent. It became too inwardly focused… And you need to know that, when you're with me, empathy and nurturing are not nice-to-haves; they're requirements. And you keep them switched on round the clock. You don't clock out when work's over."

Goran was again slightly stunned by Selveta's assertiveness. But it was admirable assertiveness. No one would challenge her diagnosis or question her fix.

"But, Goran, I promise you that this will be your liberation. Instead of setting all those high internal hurdles, push all that goodness out to other people around you. You bathe your patients in a warmth that's a privilege to witness. Now do that to me. We were friends before but you kept me at arm's length. Now I'm taking a step in. Things will change… for the better. You'll see."

Selveta smiled and laid both her hands on his hands. Her little lecture was complete. She had supplied him with the manual of how to live the rest of his life – the short version. Did it feel daunting? No, not really. Might he be capable of switching off the incessant internal questions; the worries about whether he was doing the right thing? Just twenty-four hours earlier he couldn't have imagined how. It would have appeared inconceivable. But now Selveta's guidance appeared to have illuminated the way with the strength of a powerful flashlight. His head whirled slightly at the prospect of having to live up to her requirements. At times it might be quite an intense ride, but the allure was irresistible: the switch from worshipping a spectre to living with a partner who would demand commitment seemed less like a challenge; more a relief – that word again.

"Goran, you need to know that what I'm *not* saying is that you can't talk about Ana or say how you're feeling about her. You can always bring her up in conversation if you're struggling with something, or even have a nice memory. In fact, what I think we should do is fly back from London to Belgrade. We can go to her grave – together. Say goodbye. And then the page is turned, and our life is in Bosnia. What do you think of that?"

Again, Goran was unclear as to whether this was a plan she had thought up some time ago or whether she had ad-libbed it on the spur of the moment, but inside he was touched by the sentiment and thrilled by the idea. "Selveta, it's kind of you to suggest that. Yes – that would be lovely."

22

Just as Torquay was the first town in England that Goran had visited, so it was with Selveta. Just as the weather had been benign when Goran had first visited, so it was for Selveta. Perhaps a slightly stronger breeze coming off the sea this time, but bright sunshine, landscape and coastal views that Selveta would never have associated with grey, rainy England.

Selveta had polished her schoolroom English to a developed stage, thanks to the time she had spent alongside World Vision staff in Tuzla, where English was the common language; so, as the two couples walked along Torre Abbey Sands, she and Sandra were able to peel off from Goran and Milan and leave them to their reflections on how the Mladić trial might play out in The Hague.

"Sorry for having to ask this, Selveta, but do I set you both up in our second double bedroom or do you need me to put you in separate rooms?" Sandra asked.

"You can put us together in the double, if that's okay," said Selveta.

"Yes, of course. I just wasn't sure… What with Ana and the letter…"

Selveta sensed that Sandra was flustered; afraid of saying something amiss, given the delicacy of the recent situation. She recalled an English saying that a former colleague used to use back in Tuzla: "When you're in a hole, Selveta, stop digging."

"It might seem a bit quick, Sandra, but to be honest, we've been 'together' for quite some time. It just needed a 'moment' to happen for us to be properly together." She paused. "And obviously, that moment was when he sent Milan the letter and hotfooted it back to Belgrade."

Selveta explained how she had read the letter to Milan before it had been sent, and how she'd taken Goran's sedatives and left him a note.

"Do you think he might have overdosed if you hadn't realised what he was up to?" Sandra asked.

Selveta paused. "On balance, no. But once I was aware of his thinking – no, I don't. I knew pretty much that, when he read my note and saw I'd taken away his tranquillisers, he'd stop in his tracks and give me a call."

And Selveta told Sandra about the large framed photo of Ana that Goran had insisted on keeping in full view in his flats in Tuzla and then Sarajevo. "When I met him off the coach the other day and we walked back to his flat, he let me in and then he went straight to the photo and put it away, face down, in a drawer. It was quite sweet, actually."

"I can imagine," said Sandra. "Sounds like the end of one chapter and the start of another."

"Precisely. I've told him it's fine to talk about Ana. She's not a banned topic or anything." Selveta paused. "But we needed a drama before he was able to move on."

"Well, obviously, I never knew Ana, but I think you two look great together." And Sandra laid her hand affectionately on Selveta's forearm.

"Thanks, Sandra. We *will* be great together. We will be." Selveta paused. "You've no reason to know it, but 'Selveta' means 'comfort' or 'consolation' in Bosnian. But I think we'll quickly move beyond the stage where I'm comforting him or consoling him about his loss – let alone being a consolation prize! We're going to go to Belgrade on our way back and visit Ana's grave. Then, as you said, it's a new chapter. We'll live in Bosnia, and before long Belgrade and Serbia will be just part of his past story. He's comfortable in Bosnia. I've seen it in him. He's got the fact that Bosnia is more – what's the word in English? – authentic. Yes, that's the word. Bosnia's more authentic than Serbia. Though I'm not sure he'd admit it quite yet."

If Goran had been looking at her, he would have seen Selveta flexing her bare toes in the sand and he would have registered just how happy she appeared to be in that moment.

"I know this might sound strange coming from a medical type, Milan." Goran realised he was adopting Selveta's vocabulary. "But I'm bothered that, at The Hague, Ratko's going to get five-star medical treatment. That shrunken, pathetic man dragged out of a tumbledown farmhouse will get strong again. He'll be given good food. He'll regain all that swagger and arrogance. He'll try to make his trial a circus – just like Slobo did."

"I agree with you, Goran," said Milan. "But, you know, part of me wants him to get well so that he can go through the trial and be convicted. I want proper justice. Not him slipping away like Milošević."

Goran and Milan had got their mutual apologies out of the way just moments after Goran and Selveta had crossed the Teševićs' threshold.

"Milan, I'm sorry for putting you in such a difficult position. I wasn't thinking straight. If I'd thought for a minute about the effect it would have on you, I would never have sent that letter. Or rather, I'd have left out the bit about trying to find a way back to Ana."

"It's okay, Goran. It's just that I wondered whether it was what they call 'a cry for help'. I didn't think the local police here would think it was any of their business. So that's why I called Mick. It was the only way I could think of getting international attention, and I knew I had to give him a strong story if he was going to write about it."

"Front-page news, Milan! You did the job! Anyone would think you were a spin doctor!" Goran grinned.

The following day *The Times* carried a two-paragraph story in a 'Brief News' column on page four under the headline 'Missing Serbian medic found safe and well'.

"I gave him a call, Goran – after his story was published and I learned that you were safe. I didn't tell him you'd be coming to England imminently. Otherwise, he'd be banging on the door, wanting your life story!"

And Goran told Milan the story of how he'd seen Mick in his and Ana's favourite café in Belgrade, and then the following day by Ana's grave and in front of the former Mladić household.

"He told me he was flying out to Belgrade, but, heavens! That's some coincidence," said Milan.

"Well, the café bit was spooky, though it is in one of the trendiest areas: Skadarlija. He'd probably booked a hotel room near there. But I've thought about it and I'm not so sure the rest is so surprising. If you think of it: two people in Belgrade on the same day, both planning to go to Ana's grave. When would you go? Mid morning, most likely – so maybe it wasn't so crazy that our paths crossed.

"Mind you, I can't tell you how much I wanted to speak to him. Of course, I didn't know he was your friend Mick. But he was clearly a journalist who had a detailed knowledge of the fall of Yugoslavia. He knew about Ana as well as about Ratko. And I wanted to get his take. But I knew that, if I did, I'd become the story: the guy they were all looking for after Ana's death. I just couldn't do it.

"I have to say, though, I thought he captured the atmosphere in the Topčider Cemetery beautifully. All those noisy headstones, and then Ana's which tells you precisely nothing but – as Mick put it so perceptively in his article – probably conceals the most poignant story in the whole estate. Nicely done, I thought."

Later that day, the two couples were sitting at a table outside The Hole in the Wall in the sunshine. Milan was explaining how fulfilled he was by teaching teenagers modern history and English literature.

"Goran, I can't believe how I ended up here, doing what I'm doing. I feel really blessed," he said.

"You deserve it, mate. You've worked hard to get here – particularly given that you arrived here with not much English. Personally, I'm looking forward to you writing your own first novel, Milan – in English. That's the next challenge for you."

"Like when am I going to get time to write a novel? I'm knocked out with work already!"

Goran sipped at his Brakspear real ale. "Come on, Milan. Aim high! Could be a story about an innocent young man who ends up working for a mass murderer and wonders how to escape his dilemma."

"Nah, nah... Too implausible," said Milan.

And they laughed.

Then Goran looked across at Selveta and he found himself all but overwhelmed by a feeling of pride in his new partner. On the English Riviera, in the sunshine, in the company of good friends – how had such a turnaround occurred just days after he had felt in the depths of despair? Selveta had taken him in hand. That was how. She had reoriented him. She had diagnosed his problem and prescribed his fix. A change of scenery, good company, and a brand-new perspective on the way ahead. She was a miracle worker. She and Sandra were getting on famously and he could feel the goodness glowing from her. She was wearing a brown sleeveless top and the wind was caressing the down on her arms. Love welled up inside him as he gazed at her.

"What are you thinking about, Goran?" Selveta asked, feeling his gaze upon her.

He broke into a smile and said simply, "Stuff!"

As they went to leave Torquay for the journey back, Goran had to stop himself from telling Milan and Sandra that they must come to his and Selveta's wedding, though he had had to miss theirs. He and Selveta were far from discussing that, though Goran felt that there was an inevitability about it. But the two couples' friendship was now established. They would be meeting up at least annually from now on, Goran expected.

Although it had cost them extra to return via Belgrade rather than buy standard return trips to Sarajevo, and although they would need an eight-hour coach journey to get back to Sarajevo, having hatched their plan to visit Ana's grave, they stuck with it. Goran wondered whether he should have volunteered to pass on this extra leg to their trip, but in the event, he held back from suggesting it because he had a hunch that perhaps part of the original proposal from Selveta was that she too might feel a need to see the grave in order for her to have a sense of completion of the Ana chapter.

They took a taxi to the east gate of the cemetery and Goran felt his usual sense of relief to find that no one was by the grave. There was a pot of crimson and white chrysanthemums that were fresh enough to have been placed on the grave within the last couple of days, so Ana still had visitors.

As they stepped alongside the grave, Goran made the sign of the cross. "Here we are, Selveta. This is it." He realised that he felt a certain pride, as if he were exhibiting to her something of his own handiwork. "You see – just like Mick said in his piece: all these portraits, all these words to try to capture the spirits of lost loved ones on all the other headstones. And Ana's – just simple. Just her." He felt a tear in his eye.

"Yes – there's something pure about it, isn't there?" said Selveta. "I get it."

They sat down on the bench and Selveta took Goran's hand. They said nothing for a few minutes. Then Selveta said, "Goran, do you mind if I ask you something? Personal?"

"No, no – of course."

"Well, in your letter to Milan you said you wanted to try to find a way back to Ana. But you don't believe in the afterlife. And when we arrived, you made the sign of the cross. Is something going on?"

"Is something going on?" Goran ran his fingers through his hair. "Crikey, Selveta, you ask good questions. I should be getting used to them by now."

Goran had to take time to think, as he had never before tried to put into words what had happened to him spiritually over the past few years. "You know, Selveta, maybe I've made a journey from my parents' absolute atheism to somewhere on the agnostic spectrum.

"I've never told anyone this before, but I'll swear that, after she died, for a good few months at least it felt like I was continuing my dialogue with Ana from beyond the grave. It was as if I could float out ideas and thoughts to her and she'd float something back. It could just be that I'd known her so well that I was sensing intuitively what she'd have said in a situation; how she'd respond to a specific point. But it sure as hell felt real. Like conversations. Proper conversations.

"But the other thing has been working alongside people like you and the Christians in the World Vision teams. I just sense that your faith and prayers and those of the World Vision Christians bestow upon you all a calmness. I can't say it hasn't affected me. Sometimes I've thought I wanted a piece of it. I *don't* want to participate in it, but I can't deny there's something real in it for you all. Maybe some time ago I would have thought it superstitious nonsense, but now I suppose I have to concede that they're valid belief systems."

"Valid belief systems!" Selveta exclaimed. "Oh, really, Mr Cool Analyst?!" She gave him a playful punch in the ribs. "They've been studied and developed over thousands of years. They're a bit more than that!"

Goran smiled and held up his hands, as if to say, *Fair cop*. "Okay, okay..."

They sat in silence for a little longer before Goran pointed out the Ada Bridge filling the gap between the trees at the top of the cemetery.

"You see that bridge, Selveta? When I first used to come here, it wasn't there, but as they've pieced it together, it's become an ever more magnificent sight. It's a beautiful piece of architecture. One of the first times it had taken on its final shape I came here shortly before closing hours and there was a fabulous sunset: orange fading into pink with inky dashes across the skyline. And I was pretty much overwhelmed."

"You mean it was a spiritual moment?" Selveta teased.

"Yes – something like that…" He appreciated her irony. "But," he went on, "and I hope this doesn't sound too highfaluting, it's now a symbol for me. You see those cables? They look like harp strings, but they reminded me of your dad's saz and that music evening we had shortly after I landed in Tuzla. And I thought you were so kind to arrange that and include me in it.

"Anyway, you may not be aware of the geography but that bridge is crossing from the east bank of the River Sava, and from this side it's leading people out of Belgrade to the west. And that's my journey. I started from here and this beautiful bridge is the symbol of my transition west… To Bosnia. To you. When I first visited Ana after she'd gone, there was no bridge. It took a painful period of time to take shape, but it's complete now. My journey – from Ana to Bosnia, to you – is complete now." Goran couldn't help some tears from trickling down his face.

"Oh, Goran. That's so lovely." Selveta leaned in and hugged him as best she could, as they sat side by side on the bench.

He wiped the tears from his face and took a few deep breaths to try to compose himself. He turned to Selveta and said, "Selveta, I know this might sound like an odd thing to ask, but it was such a special moment for me, that day in Čaklovići Gornji when you sang for Elvedin. You wouldn't sing the song about Jahora's mountain for me, would you?"

"What? Now?"

"Yes. Now. Here."

Selveta was momentarily stunned by the request; then Goran sensed her move towards a 'hell, why not?' moment. "Oh… Okay, then."

Just as she had done in the field above that little hamlet a few years earlier, she rang out the notes boldly, drifting them out across headstones and grave slabs, like an unexpected angel descending and blessing the dead with her song.

Oh, how big is Jahora's mountain?...
The grey falcon cannot fly over it...

Goran thrilled to his core at the sweetness of the notes and at her public performer's confidence in casting her song as far as it would carry.

The young girl ran over it without a horse...
Bosnian women comb their red hair.

As the final notes died on the air, a smattering of applause could be heard from somewhere out of sight. Six Little Sisters of Jesus appeared. They had been cleaning the tomb containing the remains of sisters who had passed away over the years – just as they had when Goran had witnessed them at work shortly after Ratko had been arrested. The nuns picked their way towards Ana's grave, curious as to the source of the song. Had Goran had Selveta's fluency in English, he would have recognised that the lead nun spoke with an Irish accent to Selveta.

"God bless you, my dear. You sing like an angel, so you do."

"Lovely – just lovely," muttered another nun behind her.

"Thank you, thank you. You're so kind," said Selveta.

The lead nun looked across at Ana's headstone. "That's a terrible thing for a girl to die so young," she said. "Was she family?" And she laid a hand compassionately on Selveta's shoulder.

"Yes, yes – she was family," said Selveta. Goran noticed how she had not so much as hesitated as she had answered the question.

"Well, we'll be praying to Mother Mary and Jesus Christ Our Lord for her soul," the lead nun said.

"Thank you," said Selveta. She acknowledged Goran. "We'll both be very grateful to you for that."

The nuns turned to go, but the lead nun had one parting comment. "And, my dear – make sure you don't keep that beautiful singing voice to yourself. The world needs to hear it. You're like an angel, so you are."

As the nuns in the sky-blue tunics and white veils slipped away, Goran and Selveta looked at each other, slightly stunned by this 'divine intervention'. They smiled at one another. There didn't seem any need for commentary.

Goran stood up and said, "Come on, Selveta. Time to go. Let's take a walk down the hill back to the city centre." At the grave's edge, he turned and said, "Ana, we'll be back", though he felt a sense of finality. And he blew a kiss in the direction of the headstone. Selveta hooked her arm inside the bow of his elbow.

As they turned towards the gate and had an even less interrupted view of the bridge, Selveta said, "I love your image of the saz – but do you know how I see it, Goran? It's a sailing ship. A ship to sail us away."

Goran took Selveta to Čolak Antina so that he could introduce her to his parents, and, as he had expected, the chemistry was powerful. He sensed that his mother and father warmed to Selveta and admired her for her commitment to the damaged children of Bosnia. He was sure they sensed the full range of her empathy. He believed they were delighted that their son had found so compelling a partner. He felt that Selveta would have appreciated intuitively the decency and integrity that underpinned their lifelong pursuit of the golden key to a compassionate political system, and, of course, the natural facility with which they had brought up Goran and his brother so expertly.

Goran and Selveta had time as well to pop in on Danijel Tešević, who was delighted to receive the latest reports of his son and daughter-in-law from the English Riviera. He had few fresh insights into developments at The Hague, but his forecast that the Mladić trial would take a long time proved to be accurate, as his forecasts always were. He was interested to hear of Goran and Selveta's work, but his prognosis for Bosnia was not encouraging.

"I find it hard to see how Bosnia can grow and thrive with the structure they've set up at Dayton. Letting the Bosnian Serbs have their own state within a state will just mean ongoing pressure for them to hook up with Belgrade and revisit the whole Greater Serbia vision. And we know how destructive that is. And with a rotating presidency every eight months, I can't see how they're going to create the consistent policies you need for the country to grow again," he said.

"Oh, Mr Tešević, I just hope we can do something to stop the brain drain; to stop all our brightest youngsters from going abroad," said Selveta.

On the coach home the following day, Selveta slipped her fingers into Goran's, laid her head on his arm and said, "Goran – you know, I've been thinking."

"Oh, yes?"

"Perhaps I was a little harsh on you for your ultimatum to Ana."

"Really?"

"Yes. Having met your parents, I can see you were raised in an environment where integrity was everything. I didn't understand it before, but I wonder whether you were so steeped in it, you couldn't imagine how other people you loved and respected could have a different take. You couldn't understand how you could say to Ana, 'Me or him', and she might come up with a different answer."

She paused. Goran hadn't processed her re-evaluation sufficiently to respond.

"Yes, I think that's it. I'm sure that's it," she said. "So, as I say, maybe I was a bit harsh in suggesting that Ana's relationship with her father wasn't really your business."

Goran was still considering how to reply when Selveta added, "They are amazing, your parents, I have to say."

"Yes, they're a bit special," he replied. "They're what I'd call compassionate Communists. They honestly believed that there was a route to a Communism run altruistically at a community level. Nothing like the Soviet Union.

"There was a guy called Edvard Kardelj – one of Tito's political theorists; one of his closest aides. And he crafted the Constitution in 1974 that aimed to achieve what was called 'the withering away of the state'. A Communist state without the bad guys, if you like!" Goran laughed. "My parents were fans of his. They really believed that a point could be reached at which the state and its dead hand would wither away.

"They'd been active, tried to influence the course of post-Tito Yugoslavia and Serbia, and then realised that not everyone was as pure and reasonable as their academic and political colleagues. And then the bad stuff began to happen, and while they were trying to find a logical, clear, altruistic political philosophy, I was lunching with Ratko. I was seeing at first hand the kind of people who were assuming power. Pardon my language, but I was seeing that it's the shits who rise to the top: Milošević, Karadžić, Mladić. And when they read the signs in the late '80s, early '90s, my parents backed out of the public debate. I remember once, Selveta, walking into the kitchen and my mum had raised her voice to my father – something she never did. She was saying they would lose their jobs and their home if they continued to maintain political profiles. After that, they hosted no more political discussions at our home. It was sad because they seemed like such intense discussions between some really clever people. I'd peer down from the stairs to try to overhear what was being said, though I was too young to understand it at first."

"I didn't realise they'd been active politically," said Selveta.

But Goran wanted to pick up on her earlier point. "To go back to what you said about the ultimatum to Ana. Initially I was really shocked when you told me I had no place in laying it down to her. That it should have been entirely her decision how to manage her relationship with her father. I think I was shocked because it preceded the pivotal moment in my life. To the extent that I felt *I* owned it. That maybe it wasn't for you or anyone else to comment on it.

"But – though I agree it was partly my upbringing that convinced me I was right to do it – looking at it now, after everything that's happened, I do think there was a lot in your original analysis. Maybe I took a step too far. I always vowed I'd never regret that ultimatum. I had to do it, I told myself. Now I'm beginning to accept that it's okay to allow a little bit of regret to creep in."

Selveta looked up at him. "Tell you what, Goran. Let's just let it slide a little, eh? You acted with integrity. You might have some regret – but let's let it slide. We don't need to pore over it all any more. Shine that light of yours outwards – not inwards." She laid her hand on his shoulder and said softly, "After all, we're on our sailing ship, heading west."

And they smiled and hugged.

23

As Milan's father had forecast, the trial of Ratko Mladić was long drawn out. The process lasted more than six years; the trial more than four years. There were 530 days of evidence and courtroom argument. Evidence from four hundred witnesses was submitted or given orally at The Hague.

Ana's father was found guilty of ten of the eleven charges brought against him. The charges on which he was convicted included genocide, crimes against humanity, extermination, murder, terror and unlawful attack, the sniping and shelling of civilians, and hostage-taking of UN military observers and peacekeepers. He was sentenced to life imprisonment.

By the time the trial was over and the verdict was announced, Goran and Selveta had been married for five years. They had a four-year-old and a two-year-old, both girls: Ismeta and Lamija.

When they met friends and family, Selveta would often say, "We'll need to complete our set", which Goran knew meant that he would have to help produce a boy before his procreative responsibilities were fulfilled. "We can't have you as the only man in a household of girls," Selveta would say to him privately with a smile.

Before their wedding Goran had had initial concerns that their desire to be together formally might be haram: proscribed by Islamic law. Under the letter of the law, the head of the household – the man – could not be an 'infidel'. And he was pretty sure he was an infidel. But when he had raised it with Selveta's father, he had reassured Goran.

"In Bosnia, we Muslims tend to wear our Islam lightly. Our faith is important to us but we're not fanatics. And I can see that my daughter wants to be with you, so, as far as I am concerned, you are welcome into our family," he had said.

Goran admitted to himself that he could have made things easier by converting to Islam. He had dipped into the Koran but he just couldn't find an entry point. The gulf between his childhood atheism and Islam was just too far, and his delicate shift in recent years to a low-grade agnosticism was not a sufficiently sturdy bridge. What's more, neither Selveta nor her father had ever even suggested he might consider it. Ismeta and Lamija would be raised as Muslims but they would wear their Islam lightly, Selveta and Goran agreed.

The wedding and celebration took place in the garden of Selveta's parents' home in Tuzla, and Goran was thrilled that Sandra and Milan could attend. Sandra was pregnant with their first child. Danijel Tešević made it too. Goran's heart was also warmed by the grace that his arch-atheist parents showed in embracing the Islamic ceremony. Their love for Selveta shone through and Goran could feel their pride as Selveta's father's group struck up and their daughter-in-law broke into song at the start of an unforgettable musical evening.

On the day of The Hague verdict, Goran sat glued to the TV, trying to take in the details as his girls pottered around the sitting room. As Goran had forecast, Ratko had shed the frail, shrunken appearance that had shocked everyone upon his arrest. Although he had ongoing medical issues, he had clearly been given the five-star medical care Goran had known he would receive at The Hague. And the boor and the bully and the swagger and the arrogance were all back in full view. There had been frequent foul-mouthed tirades, some of which saw him banished from the courtroom – not least as the verdict was being read out. He had to be removed before the full details could be announced.

As the verdict concluded with Ratko convicted of genocide at Srebrenica plus a string of other charges, and a life sentence was issued, Goran clenched his raised fists in the air and shouted, "Yes!" If it felt a little understated, it was the only instinctive reaction he could muster.

He called Milan in Torquay, and the two men, who had first met when on different sides of the Mladić debate, were united in their joy at seeing the man go down.

"Goran, I was so scared when I landed at your flat that night. My only hope was that no one would have noticed I'd gone, because I knew that, if he knew I'd done a runner, I'd be dead meat," said Milan.

"Well, tonight, Milan, though we're miles apart, let's raise a glass to The Hague… and to Ana," said Goran. And he thought it, but he didn't say it: *To Ana, who was collateral damage in her father's rampage through contemporary history.*

Then Goran found himself imagining that he was back in the sitting room at Blagoja Parovića 119 and he was looking at Ratko's shelf of great Russian literature; his volumes of military history. He was recalling his initial realisation that there was a brilliance in there beneath the murderous monster. And Goran asked himself – not for the first time, but the first time in a long time – whether a very different Ratko might have developed had his father, Neđa, survived long enough to raise him through childhood. Ana had had no stories handed down to her of the grandfather she had never known, and Goran had never had a sufficiently close relationship with Ratko's wife, Bosa, to be able to probe her about any indications of the kind of man he might have been. He had passed on his bravery to his elder son, undoubtedly, but might he have been a compassionate man; a man with decency who could have nipped in the bud any dysfunctional inclinations in Ratko and taught him respect and compassion for others? The family's rank poverty didn't decree that their behaviour be brutal. There were plenty of poor, gentle people. So had Ratko missed out a critical step in his personal education?

It was another of Goran's challenging, unanswerable questions. It rattled around inside him for a while. Then his girls were pulling at his legs and his attention was drawn elsewhere – just like any other 'normal' father to two small children.

Later that day, with his daughters packed off to bed, the news bulletins ran – on endless repeat – clips of the conviction of Ratko and of the ugly scenes as he had sworn at the judges and been bundled out of the dock. Not surprisingly, Goran's thoughts kept drifting back to Ana. For a moment he wanted to unclip the catches on the trunk underneath the bed and take another look at his framed photograph of her, but he resisted the temptation, as he reflected on this Bosnian life he had cooperated in constructing around himself. Sarajevo – a magical, cosmopolitan, dazzling city where no one cared whether an infidel had married a Muslim woman. This wife, these children he could never have imagined. But what would life have been like had Ana lived?

When he peered into his past and his heart, he couldn't envisage any circumstances in which he would have let her go, and he didn't believe she would have let him go. So they would have been together – not here in Sarajevo, but here now. Would he have been a different person within? How might he have lived his life had he not had Selveta to help map out a new way of living, of thinking, of loving?

And another difficult question descended out of the blue. Now that Ratko was out of the way, out of his life, might he take his girls at some point when they were older to Topčider and explain this piece of his backstory to them? And if he concealed it, what if it were to emerge later, like a scandal he had kept from them?

But all these questions were just too hard to answer, and if occasionally they still dogged him and tried to torment him, Selveta had taught him that not every question needed to be pursued to its logical end. Not every question *could* be pursued to its logical end. It was okay to let some of those questions swirl around and then lie down.

Selveta had stepped back into the sitting room and was asking about their plans for the children the following day. And as his own questions subsided within him, he recalled Selveta saying to him, the day after they had visited Topčider together, "Goran, shine that light of yours outwards – not inwards."

And he stood up, walked across to her and, without answering the practical questions she had just asked him, he put his arms around her, pressed his lips to her temple firmly and held them there, and he realised that, while she wouldn't know precisely what he was thinking, she would feel cherished.

ACKNOWLEDGEMENTS

I would have been unlikely to have researched in depth the fall of Yugoslavia had it not been for a visit I made to Sarajevo as a political journalist with the then Prime Minister, John Major, in 1996 – just months after the end of the near four-year siege. How could it be that this multi-cultural, multi-ethnic European city had been besieged for so long without meaningful intervention by 'the West'? By the time I arrived, virtually every pane of glass in the city-centre had been shot out. How was this acceptable, when west of the Balkans, it would never have been tolerated for a week, let alone four years?

If that visit to Sarajevo made a huge impression on me, two books in particular reinforced my fascination with the conflicts that led to the break-up of the Yugoslav Federation: Misha Glenny's *The Fall of Yugoslavia*, and Ed Vulliamy's *The War is Dead, Long Live the War*. Both had a profound effect on me, and I would recommend them to any reader. Julian Borger's *The Butcher's Trial* was also an important source of information contained in my novel – a forensic analysis of the demise and capture of Ratko Mladić.

I am also profoundly grateful to the late Paddy Ashdown, the former leader of the Liberal Democrats and former High Representative for Bosnia and Hercegovina. Just three months before his death in 2018 he shared with me his insights into the conflicts and into the character and behaviours of Ratko Mladić. I also mined David Owen's book, *Balkan Odyssey*, for his experiences and view of the Bosnian Serb Commander-in-Chief. Milo Jelesijević's *Ratko Mladić – Criminel ou Héros* was another important source of stories, commentary and interviews with Mladić. I have tried to capture as many authentic details and as much informed analysis as possible in this book.

I would also like to thank my daughter Alice, my best friend Ray Hedley, and all others who offered thoughts and comments on passages of this novel as I worked it up.

I would also like to acknowledge the warmth of welcome, help and advice from individuals I met across Croatia, in Belgrade and, in particular, across Bosnia during my travels and research. Bosnia especially will always have a special place in my heart. It is a largely unknown jewel at the heart of Europe whose people paid a high price for the Western world's prevarications.

This book is printed on paper from sustainable sources managed under the Forest Stewardship Council (FSC) scheme.

It has been printed in the UK to reduce transportation miles and their impact upon the environment.

For every new title that Troubador publishes, we plant a tree to offset CO_2, partnering with the More Trees scheme.

MORE TREES
LET'S PLANT A BILLION TREES

For more about how Troubador offsets its environmental impact, see www.troubador.co.uk/sustainability-and-community